SURVIVORS

FIRE: CHICAGO, 1871

VORS

FIRE: CHICAGO, 1871

KATHLEEN DUEY

and KAREN A. BALE

Aladdin

New York   London   Toronto   Sydney   New Delhi

ALADDIN

An imprint of Simon & Schuster Children's Publishing Division
1230 Avenue of the Americas, New York, NY 10020
This Aladdin paperback edition March 2014
Text copyright © 1998 by Kathleen Duey and Karen A. Bale
Cover illustration copyright © 2014 by David Palumbo
All rights reserved, including the right of reproduction in whole or in part in any form.
ALADDIN is a trademark of Simon & Schuster, Inc., and related logo
is a registered trademark of Simon & Schuster, Inc.
Also available in an Aladdin hardcover edition.
For information about special discounts for bulk purchases, please contact Simon & Schuster
Special Sales at 1-866-506-1949 or business@simonandschuster.com.
The Simon & Schuster Speakers Bureau can bring authors to your live event.
For more information or to book an event contact the Simon & Schuster Speakers Bureau
at 1-866-248-3049 or visit our website at www.simonspeakers.com.
Cover designed by Jeanine Henderson
Interior designed by Tom Daly
The text of this book was set in Berling LT Std.
Manufactured in the United States of America 0214 OFF
2 4 6 8 10 9 7 5 3 1
Library of Congress Control Number 97-52937
ISBN 978-1-4424-9054-3 (pbk)
ISBN 978-1-4424-9055-0 (hc)
ISBN 978-1-4424-9056-7 (eBook)

For the women
who taught us the meaning of courage:
Erma L. Kosanovich
Katherine B. Bale
Mary E. Peery

Chapter One

Nate Cooper swung the empty milk pail as he walked down Canal Street. It was a warm, breezy morning, and he was glad to be out of his Sunday suit. Aunt Ruth always made him go to church. This morning, aptly enough, the preacher had done a whole sermon on hellfire and brimstone.

The air was still filled with the acrid smell of smoke from the fire the night before. With the breeze coming from the southwest, that was a blessing. Usually when the wind came from this direction, it carried the heavy stench of the Union Stockyards.

Pushed by the light wind, ashes drifted aimlessly along the ground. Last night's fire had been a bad one—the worst one yet. A slat-ribbed horse pulling a salvage wagon clopped past. The horse and the driver looked exhausted.

"Hey, Nate!"

Nate turned. Ryan Wilson was standing on the corner of Washington Street, hands on his hips. He must have managed to slip away from his father's livery stable. Usually, his whole Sunday was spent mucking stalls. Nate waited for Ryan to catch up with him, then they fell into step.

"Did your aunt let you go watch the fire last night?" Ryan picked up a cinder and threw it across the street. Water from the pump engines, black and foul, stood stagnant in the gutter.

"Not exactly."

Ryan laughed.

"I didn't go out for long," Nate admitted. "If she checks on me and I'm not in my room, she gets worried."

Ryan glanced at him. "Was it as bad as they say? My father was concerned for a while. Thought we might have to get the horses out."

Nate let Ryan stare eagerly into his face for a few more seconds, then he nodded. "I climbed some lady's roof on Madison Street. The lumberyards and the Lull & Holmes Planing Mill went up like a bon-fire. The coal yards looked hot enough to melt iron."

Ryan kicked at a charred board. "I could hear the engines clanging almost all night. I guess the police had a hard time holding the crowds back."

Nate nodded, gesturing. A mounted policeman rode along the edge of last night's burn. His horse was a tall bay with a wide blaze. It reminded Nate of one of Ryan's father's geldings—a spirited animal Nate rode every chance he got. Sometimes Ryan's father needed help exercising the horses that were boarded at his livery stable. Once in a while, he even paid Nate to ride them.

The policeman was turning people aside. Compared to the night before, the area was almost deserted—but it wouldn't be for long. A few blocks down, Nate could see people crossing the Adams Street Bridge. Now that church was out, there would be more coming to gawk at the places where the plank streets had burned through, collapsing to the soil ten or twelve feet below.

"Gee whiz, look at that!"

Nate followed Ryan's gesture. The viaduct was a wreck. All the wooden timbers supporting the roadway above the railroad tracks had burned and fallen. The metal structure below was twisted, bent every which way. On the far side of the viaduct, the fire had destroyed everything, even the boardwalks. The rank soil beneath them had been dried out by the fire.

Now that the raised boardwalks and plank streets had been burned away, it was strange to see the exposed stone foundations of the buildings. Even the rocks were stained with smoke and split from the heat. Aunt Ruth had told him that ground level in this part of town had been raised eight feet back in the fifties and sixties, just to get it up above the sea of mud. All of Chicago had been built on a marsh, and the city workers had used dirt dredged up out of the river bottom, lifting the old buildings with jacks, a few inches at a time.

As the boys picked their way across the railroad tracks east of the collapsed viaduct, Nate slid on the chunks of charred wood that graveled the ground. "The paper-box factory nearly exploded, it went up so fast," he said over his shoulder.

"I wish I could have seen it." Ryan's voice was wistful as he caught up.

Nate led the way up the slope, crossed the railroad tracks, then went back down. Abruptly, without meaning to, he stopped, stunned. Ryan stood beside him, and for a few moments, neither one of them said a word. The fire had erased a whole neighborhood.

"You can't even see where some of the houses *were*," Ryan whispered.

Nate glanced at him, then looked back at the blackened jumble of wood and ash that had been homes, saloons, lumberyards, and factories the day before. Staring at the destruction made Nate feel strange. Last night, the fire had been beautiful. This was so ugly he felt almost sick. Behind them, he heard a woman weeping, saying something over and over in a voice so distorted her words were impossible to understand.

"Let's get out of here," Ryan said quietly.

Without answering, Nate began to walk, swinging the bucket again. He led the way, veering eastward, cutting through the destroyed neighborhood slantwise, avoiding the worst of the wreckage and the piles of still smoking timber. Once they were on the far side, where the houses still stood and the planked

5

streets were only dusted with ash, he slowed down.

"It came close to us," Ryan whispered.

Nate didn't answer. He tried to shake off the eerie feeling that had taken hold of him. "I have to go all the way down to O'Learys'. My aunt wants milk for the boarders."

"That's clear down on De Koven Street, isn't it? The place behind McLaughlins' house? Doesn't that lady drive a milk wagon?"

Nate climbed the steps up onto the boardwalk. "My aunt says O'Learys' milk is cleaner than most— she almost never finds cow hair or flecks of hay in it. But Mrs. O'Leary won't deliver on Sundays."

Ryan whistled through his teeth. "You still have that bald man, don't you? The one who—"

"Drinks half a gallon of milk a day." Nate nodded. "Mr. Dwight. Aunt Ruth has tried to make him cut down, but he won't." Nate shrugged as he went down three steps where the boardwalk changed levels. "He pays his room and board on time, he's quiet, and he gets along with all the other boarders just fine."

Ryan laughed. "That's because they don't have to pay his milk bill."

Nate grinned. "Aunt Ruth likes him. He's been

there longer than I have. And he brings her lace and notions from the dry goods where he works."

"Why don't you tell him he can only have a pint of milk a day?" Ryan asked, narrowing his eyes.

Nate saw Ryan's mouth twitching. "You know why. He weighs as much as a draft horse and he has arms like piano legs."

Ryan nodded somberly, turning to walk backward, facing Nate. "It's all the milk he drinks. This is the kind of dilemma that has no answer, Nate."

"That's true," Nate agreed, grinning again. He swung the bucket in a high arc over his head, then brought it back down.

"Can you get out again tonight?" Ryan asked, turning around to walk beside Nate again.

Nate shrugged. "I'm not the one who has trouble getting out."

Ryan stopped abruptly, just in front of the next set of steps. "I'll meet you on the corner of Clinton and Randolph at nine o'clock. Will your aunt be in bed by then?"

Nate nodded. "Sure. But if I take all morning getting the milk, she'll be after me the rest of the day. I still have a lot of chores to finish."

Ryan ran down the steps and waited for Nate. "Even on Sunday? Doesn't she keep Sabbath?"

Nate swung the pail again. "She says a boarding-house has to be run every day of the week. It won't run itself and it never closes."

Ryan wasn't listening. "Race you to the corner," he said over his shoulder, already two steps ahead. Nate sprinted after him, forgiving Ryan for cheating. He never won anyway.

Chapter Two

"Julie, will you come in and talk to me for a moment, please?"

Reluctantly, Julie looked up from her book. She had run out of her favorite dime novels—the exciting stories about the West she and her father loved—and had begun this new *Elsie Dinsmore* novel. She had expected to be bored, but she wasn't. Martha Farquharson was becoming one of her favorite authoresses.

"Julie Flynn, do you hear me?"

Julie laid her book aside and leaned back in the overstuffed chair. She ran her hand along the red velvet cushion, trying to ignore her mother's voice from the parlor. She glanced up at her father. He was sitting in his worn leather chair, reading his newspaper.

Julie loved Sundays because she was allowed to spend quiet time with her father in the library. Usually it was peaceful. This Sunday was different. Her mother was agitated and pacing the carpet in the parlor. Julie wished she had never asked permission to go with her father. She should have known how her mother would react.

"You'd best go talk to your mother, Julie," her father said.

"Why does she have to make such a fuss? I just want to go down to the Cass Street store with you." Julie didn't look at her father directly. She pulled at her sleeve, tracing a bright yellow strand of the plaid pattern. Then she glanced up through her lashes.

Her father shrugged, a discouraged look on his face. "Your mother is so upset. Maybe you should just do as she says tonight."

Julie shook her head. "I always do as she says."

Her father winked. "She only worries for you because she loves you."

Julie nodded quickly. She didn't want to hear him defend her mother. She had heard it a thousand times.

She was her parents' only child, and her mother was high-strung and anxious by nature. Since July, there had been at least one fire somewhere in the city almost every week—Julie's mother had been fluttery and short-tempered for months.

Julie met her father's eyes. "Please, talk to her. I'll just sit in the wagon. Tell her that."

"I will try once more, Julie. But after the fire last night—"

"There will be fires until it rains," Julie interrupted him. "Everybody knows that." Julie watched her father's face darken.

"If your mother hears you say that, she'll have me standing fire watch atop the roof until Christmas." He reached out and touched her cheek. "I have to get more groceries down to the parish below Vernon Park. What we took to St. Paul's this afternoon isn't going to be enough. The families who got burned out last night weren't well-off to begin with. Most of them haven't got a penny left in this world."

"Please ask one more time," Julie pleaded. "I know the fires have scared Mother, but she hasn't let me go anywhere lately."

Julie's father looked at her. "I've been thinking

that maybe you should go to school, Julie. We could get rid of that dandy your mother hires to tutor you and—"

"Do you think Mother would let me?" Julie asked quickly. The idea of facing a room full of strange children made her nervous, but it was exciting, too. She had never been in a classroom. Every morning she watched girls walking arm in arm along Michigan Avenue on their way to school—and envied them. When Julie's father didn't answer her, she sighed. "I just want to go with you tonight. Please."

"I'll go talk to your mother." He touched her cheek again. "But as upset as she is, I can't promise anything."

Julie watched her father leave the room. Then she slid out of the overstuffed chair and went to the window. She pulled back the lace curtains and looked out. It was getting dusky. The tops of the birches that lined the street were arching away from the wind. The brownish water close to the river mouth was choppy; farther out, Lake Michigan was bluer, and she could see little wind-crests of white foam.

Julie crossed to the west-facing window and looked down at her mother's flower garden, then past it, toward the stables. What she really wanted to do was to have the groom saddle one of the horses and go riding. Riding with her father was one of her favorite things. He was proud of how well she could sit a horse. But there was no point in bringing up riding alone—especially now, this close to dark.

Julie stared out the window. The streets below were dotted with carriages—a lot of people had attended late Sunday services. In spite of the rising wind, it would be a perfect, warm, wonderful evening to be outside.

Julie heard her parents' voices get louder as they came back down the hall. She sprang away from the window and ran to her chair. By the time her mother sailed through the doorway, Julie pretended to be reading. She looked up, an expression of startled innocence on her face.

Julie's mother was wearing her blue moiré gown, the deep green train falling from her bustle to the floor in draped waves, the hemline edged with flounces. The balayeuse ruffle that protected the expensive train from dragging the floor was dyed to complement the watery, shining blue of the gown. As always, her mother was an image of fashionable correctness.

Julie waited, knowing better than to say anything. Her mother was flushed, fanning herself. "I don't approve of this at all, young lady. But your father insists that smoke-filled air and filthy streets will somehow be good for your health. So put on your cloak and gloves and change to your woolen stockings."

Julie bit her lip to keep from arguing about the stockings. She shot her father a grateful look as she ran out of the library and turned down the long hall. Lifting her skirts to turn the corner, Julie made a long-practiced slide on the polished wood floor, grabbing the door handle at the last moment to pull herself into her room.

Once inside, she sat on the edge of her bed and looked around. Her mother had insisted on decorating it in the new, green-stained wood, a copy of the famous Morris & Co. styles from England. The one traditional touch was Julie's quilt. It had been handed down through her mother's family for four generations. Julie hated it. Her mother was so afraid she would stain or tear it that Julie had to fold it back every time she wanted to lie on her bed to read or rest during the day.

Leaning forward, Julie hurriedly rolled off her cotton stockings and put on her thick woolen ones. The wool itched against her skin, and she knew it would only get worse as the evening went on—but it was a small price to pay. She stepped back into her shoes, wriggling her toes as she fastened the buttons. Her cloak and gloves were pressed and ready on the cloak tree beside her door.

Back in the hallway, Julie walked more slowly, her head held high, her posture ladylike. She could hear her mother in the library, her tone less shrill now, and her father's reassuring murmur. Julie hesitated in the hall, listening.

"We don't have to depend on the volunteers anymore, Margaret," her father was saying. "These men are salaried professionals. They're trained as firemen. Chicago is a much safer city now that we have them."

Julie could tell her mother was pacing the floor. The moiré silk of her gown was stiff enough to make a *swooshing* sound when she walked. "What's taking her so long?"

Startled, Julie straightened her bodice and went through the door, a little breathless and embarrassed to have been eavesdropping on her parents. She kept her eyes demurely down, trying to avoid her mother's probing glances.

"Ready?" Julie's father put his hands on her shoulders and nudged her back out of the library, guiding her along as they turned the opposite way down the wide hall. Julie could hear her mother's gown rustling as she followed them to the top of the stairway, then stopped.

Julie and her father continued on, the thick carpet erasing the sound of their footsteps as they descended. The carved banister shone, reflecting the gas lights set high on the wall.

"Good-bye, Mother," Julie called out, turning back just inside the front door.

Her mother was still hovering at the top of the stairs. She looked nervous, a smile tugging uneasily at the corners of her mouth. "You listen to everything your father tells you."

Her father mumbled a response, moving toward the heavy mahogany doors, his hands still firm on Julie's shoulders. She avoided catching her mother's eye. She knew from long experience that it might set off a torrent of parting advice. She glanced up at her father instead, hoping he would say something.

"Don't worry, Margaret," he said to his wife. "We'll be home by nine at the latest."

Chapter Three

Nate put the last load of kindling in the box. Aunt Ruth liked to mix wood with the shavings and sawdust she bought from the lumberyard. It made the stove fire brighter and less smoky.

"Oh, my goodness," she said, bustling up behind him. "I almost forgot the pies. I sometimes wonder where my mind wanders off to." She set the pie tins on her pastry table.

Nate smiled, knowing that if he hadn't been there, she would have had the same conversation with herself. "Your mind is on twenty things at once, Aunt Ruth."

She beamed at him, wrinkles creasing her cheeks. She was really his great-aunt, his grandmother's sister.

When his parents had died in the cholera epidemic in St. Louis, he had been placed in St. Michael's Boys' Orphan Asylum. Like every other asylum in the city, it was strained to bursting during the awful outbreak of the fever.

Nate had braved the gamut of bullies and stark, lonely nights for only a month before running away. For a year he had made his own way, working as a sidewalk sweep. When he couldn't find work he passed the days along the docks, dodging among the stacked crates and bins of cotton and fruit. He had crept into stables or storage sheds to sleep most nights, shivering and hungry.

Then, two years ago, Aunt Ruth had gotten tired of exchanging letters with St. Louis agencies that claimed her great-nephew had disappeared for good. She hired a man to find him. Nate had been afraid on the long train ride, sitting next to the mustached stranger who had pulled him kicking and screaming from beneath a garbage bin. Nate had stood in his tattered, too-small clothes at the Chicago station, terrified. But Aunt Ruth had taken him in without question.

It had been hard at first, trying to live by her rules, but it hadn't taken him long to realize how much he had missed having a home. Nate was twelve now and big for his age, thanks to Aunt Ruth's kindness and good cooking. Most of the time, he obeyed her. And when he didn't, she was kindly even when she was upset with him.

"You got a little soot on the windowsill coming in last night," Aunt Ruth said abruptly, no longer smiling. "Where did you go?"

Nate ducked his head. "I just wanted to see if the fire was coming close."

Aunt Ruth was looking at him when he glanced up. "If you would spend as much time studying your books as you do studying everything else, you'd be the top scholar in your class."

Nate pretended to rearrange the kindling, knowing he was in for a lecture. Aunt Ruth spooned pieces of sizzling fried chicken out of the skillet and into a deep bowl. "Mr. Dobbs dropped in yesterday while you were out carousing with your friends. He told me you have been absent four times in the last two weeks."

"Yes, ma'am." Nate knew better than to argue or to try to fib. Aunt Ruth never lectured him without ample evidence and a fully developed case.

She set the bowl down on the sideboard. "Nathan,

you are a smart boy. I could drop dead tomorrow, you know that. I am fifty-eight years old. The bank still owns this house. I have left it to you in my will, but how are you going to run it if you don't learn to cipher and write?"

"I can write."

"Not well enough. Nor do you cipher as accurately as you should."

Nate shook his head stubbornly. "I hate school. Mr. Dobbs's classes are boring."

Aunt Ruth leaned forward, her palms pressed against the smooth wooden kitchen table. "You're bored because you put nothing into it. Why would you expect to get something out? Nothing in this life is free, Nathan Cooper."

Nate met her eyes. He hated it when she was upset with him. But she didn't understand. School was hard for him. He felt out of place. Most of the other boys seemed so young, so sheltered. "I will try harder," he said out loud.

Aunt Ruth's frown dissolved into her habitual smile. "I hope you do, Nathan. I want you to have a good life." She handed him a potato masher and made a shooing motion with one hand. "Now get to work. I also want to have supper on the table in ten minutes."

Nate nodded. He poured the steaming potato water into a crock. Aunt Ruth would use it later for soup stock. He beat the potatoes into a mound of fluffy white and added a little milk and enough pepper to speckle the top. He stirred the pepper in, making sure there were no lumps at all before he spooned the potatoes into the serving dish. He could feel Aunt Ruth watching him out of the corner of her eye as she worked.

"Go ahead and carry those out. The table is already set. Ring the supper bell while you're out there, will you?"

"Is Mr. Oliver going to eat with us?"

Aunt Ruth shrugged. "His eyes were near swollen shut this morning, his wife said. And his ankle is worse. I hope he can come downstairs and join us."

Nate went through the door into the dining room. The rich oak tabletop was covered with a thick linen cloth. The table had belonged to Aunt Ruth's mother; it was her prize possession, the only real heirloom she owned. Nate set down the potatoes, remembering the first time he had eaten supper at this table. It had seemed huge, a mile long, surrounded with people he didn't know. Now, he loved the conversations, the political arguments among the men—even Mrs. Oliver's soft, insistent voice smoothing things out.

The dinner bell was on a high shelf above the mantel. It had been so warm this fall they had only built a few fires. They wouldn't need one this evening, either; the day had been hot.

Nate rang the bell loudly, facing the stairs. Then he opened the door into the little front parlor. It was stuffy from being closed up all day long. Sometimes after supper, the boarders would spend a few hours playing cards, drinking coffee, and talking.

Voices at the top of the stairs made Nate look up. Mr. Dwight was coming down slowly, every step heavy, deliberate. Behind him, his tall, thin form almost completely hidden, Mr. Thomas was talking to the Olivers. Mr. Oliver's face was pink, and his eyes were still swollen; he limped down the stairs leaning heavily on the banister, his wife hovering just behind him.

"Nate, my boy," Mr. Dwight called out. "Did you bring some fresh milk up from O'Learys' this morning?"

Nate suppressed a smile. "Yes, sir, I did. Aunt Ruth has it in the icebox now."

Mr. Dwight grinned. "It's a long walk for you, but I surely do appreciate it."

Nate nodded and sighed, pretending to be tired. "I had to wait while they unloaded a wagon full of hay, and that milk bucket is so heavy that—"

"Oh, don't let him make you feel sorry for him, Mr. Dwight," Aunt Ruth interrupted, coming through the kitchen door. She carried the big bowl full of fried chicken to the table. Mr. Thomas helped her set it down.

"Oh, look at that," Mrs. Oliver cried out, touching her husband's shoulder. "Fried chicken. That's Brian's favorite, isn't it, Brian?"

Nate made his way across the dining room while Mr. Oliver made some polite answer and Aunt Ruth invited them all to sit down. The familiar scraping of chairs and conversation followed Nate into the kitchen. When he came out again, carrying the gravy boat and a bowl of tender green beans, Aunt Ruth passed him. "I'll just get the biscuits. You go ahead and sit down."

As Nate set the food in the center of the table,

Mrs. Oliver made another of her polite exclamations. Nate took his place next to Aunt Ruth's chair at the end of the table, across from Mr. Thomas. As always, Mr. Thomas wore an impeccably neat suit and waistcoat, his conductor's watch and chain carefully polished. The other end chair was reserved for Mr. Dwight. He had been here the longest.

"Mr. Dwight?" Aunt Ruth laid the biscuit plate beside the potatoes, then sat down. "Will you say grace for us?"

Mr. Dwight cleared his throat. "Thank you, Lord, for seeing Mr. Oliver through his ordeal last night. Please bless him and all the other firemen of this great city and keep them safe. I know You are watching over those who lost their homes and loved ones in the fire. And if You could look into a little rain for us, it would be most gratefully received. We humbly ask Your blessing upon this supper and everyone at this table. Amen."

"Amen." Nate echoed with the others. He loaded his plate with food, trying to keep from staring at Mr. Oliver. His face was so pink, it looked scalded. His eyes were slits between puffy lids. His wife doted on him, making sure he got his favorite piece of chicken and that he took enough gravy to cover his biscuits and potatoes.

Mr. Thomas passed the biscuit plate. "If you don't mind telling us, Mr. Oliver, what was it like out there last night?"

"If the ladies will forgive my language, it was hellish," Mr. Oliver said without hesitation.

Nate leaned forward. He liked Mr. Oliver. Being a fireman was exciting work, and dangerous.

"We call that district the Red Flash," Mr. Oliver went on. "It's one of the worst parts of town for fire. Think about it. The streets are all planked; every block down there is full of woodworks and coal yards. Not to mention the houses—they're all wood frame and most of them are old. And if it had jumped the river into Conley's Patch—"

"Did you see the paper-box factory when it caught on fire?" Nate interrupted. "Sparks flew straight up." Aunt Ruth shot him a quick look, and he pretended not to notice.

Mr. Oliver turned. "I did, Nate. It was like the Fourth of July for a few minutes. They tell me the rooftop sitters actually cheered. Fools."

Nate looked down. He hadn't cheered, but it

had been thrilling to see the red streamers shooting upward in the dark sky.

"I will never understand why people love to watch the fires," Mrs. Oliver said in her high, breathy voice. Nate avoided Aunt Ruth's eyes again, staring fixedly at Mr. Oliver. The fireman swallowed a mouthful of food, then looked up at his wife.

Mr. Dwight cleared his throat. "Why not? If you're far enough away, it's exciting. It's not the crowd's fault that there hasn't been enough rain this year."

"The *Tribune* has run a dozen articles about the fire hazard," Mr. Thomas put in. "If they could get the Common Council to listen to them—"

"They would have to rebuild much of the city to make any real difference," Mr. Oliver broke in. "If the drought and the winds keep up, they may have little choice. Last night's fire is still a bed of hot coals in some places."

"But nobody can stop the fires, can they?" Nate asked.

"Chief Williams has all but begged the Council to put more money into new and bigger engines. I saw enough frayed hoses and worn fittings last night to make me wonder if anyone cares at all whether the whole damn place burns down."

"Oh, Brian, please don't curse."

Mr. Oliver patted his wife's hand and put his attention back on his plate. Mr. Thomas fell silent, too. Nate waited, wishing he could ask more questions, but Aunt Ruth sent him another of her sharp glances.

"All this talk about fire is so upsetting," Mrs. Oliver said to no one in particular.

Mr. Dwight made a sympathetic sound deep in his throat. "With any luck, we'll have rain soon."

"I was scheduled to work tonight," Mr. Thomas said, refolding his napkin. "A sleeper train to Milwaukee. But so much coal was lost down there that they've delayed until they can see what's what."

Outside, one of the shutters slipped free of its bracket and banged against the side of the house. Nate stood up. "I'll fasten it," he told his aunt. She nodded.

Nate went through the little parlor, then out the front door. The dry wind slapped at him, and he looked up at the stars, then back at the city. In this wind, a fire would be almost impossible for the firemen to put out.

◇ ◇ ◇

The wind whipped Julie's hair across her face as she came out the door into the alley. She liked the Cass Street store. It was smaller than some of the others her father owned, but the building was new and it smelled of clean, fresh lumber.

Her arms ached from carrying the ten-pound sacks of flour out to the wagon. She didn't complain. Her father had been working like a demon, loading tins of coffee and sugar, then fifty-pound sacks of potatoes he stacked near the front of the wagon. She was piling the flour sacks near the rear gate, placing the bags as far up onto the wagon bed as she could.

"Watch your dress," her father said, glancing sideways at her. "Your mother will have my head if you ruin it."

Julie nodded and tried to walk a little faster. Her father was restacking the flour sacks up near the driver's bench, his movements smooth and practiced. He had driven a delivery wagon for five years before he had opened his first grocery.

Julie watched her father straighten his back and pull a handkerchief from his jacket pocket. He wiped his face. "It's still warm out, even now with the sun almost down."

Julie faced into the wind so that her hair streamed out behind her. "It feels so good to be out tonight."

Her father laughed. "Maybe you can come help in the Polk Street store tomorrow. I still have one clerk out sick there. And I want to keep an eye on that new manager. I am not quite sure I trust him entirely."

Julie looked up at him. "Do you think he would steal from you?"

"Probably not." Her father squared up a stack of sugar bags, then he looked at her. "But the man is careless. I found three sacks of spoiled oats in the storeroom. They had gotten wet from a roof leak. Maybe you could help out down there for the next week or so."

Julie grinned. "Could I?" She loved working in her father's stores, but her mother almost never allowed it. She thought that shop work was too common, and that it was beneath Julie to wait on the cooks and housekeepers who came to buy groceries for their employers' kitchens.

Staring at her father's thoughtful frown, Julie shook her head. Her mother wouldn't let her. "I have lessons tomorrow anyway, Father. And Mother wants me to begin reading that book on etiquette."

Her father moved a few more flour sacks to the front of the wagon. "I want you to grow up to be a proper lady, but it's not right for you to stay in that house all the time."

Julie nodded. "But Mother—"

"I know," her father interrupted. "Your mother worries about everything. I don't want you exposed to improper influences any more than she does. But you must learn something about life." He looked up at the hazy sky, then smiled at her. "This would have taken me a lot longer if you hadn't come along."

"I like helping you, Father."

"You're good at it, too. Mrs. Hansen was telling me how you helped her carry her groceries out to her wagon."

Julie grinned, as she always did when her father complimented her. She went to get another sack of flour.

"Just bring that one, and then let's load some beans and maybe some fresh bread," her father called after her. "Lots of these women aren't going to have a place to cook for a while."

Julie started bringing the brown paper bags of beans, handing them to her father so he could arrange them neatly up against the flour. When the wagon was full of groceries, Julie's father boosted her onto the bench.

He backed the wagon around, turning to go down the alley. Once they were out on Cass Street, he whipped the team into a spanking trot. It was getting dusky; the lamplighters would soon make their rounds. Julie pushed her hair back from her face and held it against the wind.

After a few minutes, Julie's father swung the team westward onto Madison Street, heading almost straight into the wind. Ahead of them, the south branch of the Chicago River flowed in a wide, dark ribbon, cutting across the city. The sky was still hazy with smoke from last night's fire.

Julie slid closer to her father as he urged the team into a canter. When they crossed Wells Street and passed into Conley's Patch, Julie gripped the edge of the driver's bench. She hated this place. As they rolled past the saloons and the shanties, her father kept the team moving fast. Men stood in the doorways, some of them drinking from bottles, others staring out into the street as though the world were a place to hate.

As the horses clopped across the Madison Street Bridge and Conley's Patch fell behind them, Julie relaxed and her father let the team slow back into a trot. Julie gathered her hair in one hand and looked down into the dark water below.

There were ships on the river. Julie could hear the sailors shouting as they worked to take down their sails. She glanced at her father. His face was stern, remote.

"What's the matter, Father?"

He seemed startled, then patted her arm. "Look."

Julie followed his gesture. There was a blackened strip of land along the far shore. "The fire?"

He nodded. "I just wish this blasted wind would die down."

Julie gripped the edge of the bench as they came off the bridge and headed toward Canal Street. Two wagons approached them going east. They were loaded with charred lumber and piles of goods so jumbled that Julie couldn't tell what they were. Her father raised a hand in greeting, but neither driver so much as looked at him.

Julie scooted closer to her father on the bench again. The wind was warm, and she rode along in silence as they turned south on Canal Street. She held her nose against the acrid, smoky smell of the burn as they drove past it, crossing Jackson Street, on down to Van Buren. Julie stared. Most of the houses had been burned to the ground, and she suddenly understood what had been in the wagons—the charred remains of houses. For an instant she imagined what it would be like to have her own home destroyed.

"Look there," her father said as he pulled the team around the sharp corner onto Taylor. "Mr. Black is still in his shop."

Julie leaned forward. She could see the lighted lamp in the bookstore window.

"I know what." Julie's father turned to smile at her. "You can go in and see what Mr. Black has to say for himself while I deliver the groceries to the parish."

Julie nodded eagerly. "I'd like that." She had known Mr. Black all her life. He was one of her father's oldest friends. He loved books and reading more than anything, and he knew the answer to almost any question.

Julie's father clucked to the team and cracked the whip high above their backs. "You can take a look at that new Jules Verne novel. What is it?"

"*Twenty Thousand Leagues Under the Sea*," she whispered excitedly. Her mother had never approved of her reading the French author's fanciful tales.

"That's the one."

Julie took a deep breath and looked up at the stars. She liked Mr. Black and she loved Jules Verne's books. This was going to be a lot more fun than unloading groceries. She felt a stab of guilt at the thought and faced her father. "Are you sure you don't need help?"

He shook his head. "There will be plenty of men there to help unload. If you like the Verne novel, I'll buy it for you."

Julie smiled at him, then narrowed her eyes as the wind spattered her with sand. The horses' hooves made a drumlike thudding on the board-covered street. It was a wild and beautiful night, and Julie kept glancing up at her father, grateful that he had talked her mother into letting her come.

Black's Bookstore was in a small and charming building that had once been a house. Mr. Black had thought about moving his business to Booksellers Row up on State Street and Washington. Julie wished he had—it would have been almost close enough for her to walk to sometimes. But Mr. Black said the rent in the north division was higher—and besides, his carriage trade customers were used to coming here.

Julie's father pulled the team to a stop. Without a word he lifted her down and escorted her to the door. Mr. Black looked up from his desk and grinned. "William! Julie! What a nice surprise. What has you out on this windy night?"

Julie's father took off his hat. "I have to deliver some charity groceries. Are you going to work late? Could Julie stay and read awhile?"

Mr. Black nodded. "Of course. I'm working on my inventory."

"I'll be going, then," Julie's father said, putting his hat back on. He turned to her. "Be quiet and let Mr. Black work."

"I will," Julie promised. She stood beside the open door as her father went out, his coattails flapping in the wind as he climbed into the wagon. He waved, then shook the reins, urging the horses forward. After the sound of their clopping hooves had faded, Julie could hear the shop signs creaking as they swung in the fierce wind.

Chapter Four

The boardinghouse was quiet except for the striking of the clock. Nate lay on his bed, his arms folded beneath his head. If he didn't get going, he would be late meeting Ryan. He sat up, glancing at his door. Aunt Ruth had told him good night just after eight thirty. The clock in the hallway had just struck nine. She would be asleep by now.

"I won't be out more than an hour," he whispered, promising himself that he wouldn't worry Aunt Ruth. "And I will go to school tomorrow no matter what." And, he thought, sliding the window upward, he would make sure there was no dirt or soot on the sill for Aunt Ruth to find in the morning. The curtains billowed inward, shoved aside by the wind.

Nate stepped up onto the wide sill. He hesitated only a moment, balancing, one hand on the swaying branch of the maple tree that grew outside his window. A few seconds later he was on the ground, the wind molding his shirt against his body. He ran, light-footed, until he was well away from the boardinghouse. Then he dropped back to a striding walk as he crossed Canal Street. Walking fast against the wind, he could see Ryan standing beside the gas lamp on the corner.

"It's about time," Ryan called in a hoarse whisper as Nate got close. "I was about to give up on you."

"I have to wait until I'm sure my aunt's asleep. I've told you that."

Ryan shrugged, nodding. "This wind is pretty strong."

Nate turned so that his hair blew back from his face. "Mr. Oliver said the fire could get started up again in a gale like this."

"You want to go down and get a look at it?"

Nate shook his head. "There's nothing down there but a bunch of black boards and piles of junk and ash. You saw it."

Ignoring Nate, Ryan began to walk down the center of Clinton Street. Nate waited a few seconds, then started after him. "All right, we'll go look. But I have to be home in an hour."

Ryan didn't answer, but he hurried. Nate kept up, enjoying the warm gusts that buffeted them. Overhead the stars were bright; the smoky haze was being blown out over Lake Michigan. They walked for a time in silence, hunched against the constant wind.

As they crossed Adams Street, entering the fire-blackened ruins, Nate remembered what Mr. Oliver had said about the people watching the fire—and it made him feel guilty. Mr. Oliver had been right. Usually, the crowds acted like it was a show, a circus meant to entertain them.

Nate looked at the collapsed viaduct, wondering for the first time how long it would take to fix it, how long it would be before anyone could live on these streets again. He raised his eyes, looking into the darkness across the river. Mr. Oliver had said Conley's Patch hadn't burned. Aunt Ruth would rejoice if it ever did. The saloons and gambling dens stood close beside the brothels and flophouses. Nate never walked through Conley's Patch alone.

They walked on, Ryan leading the way. Nate

shoved his hands into his pockets, his stomach tight and uneasy. Looking at the fire wreckage was worse now than it had been this morning. In the murky darkness, everything looked eerie. Here and there a timber stood canted to one side, swinging at an angle in the wind. They crossed Harrison Street, passing the edge of the burn, stepping back up onto the undamaged plank boardwalk.

"You going to school tomorrow?" Ryan asked without turning.

"I'd better. Aunt Ruth is about at wit's end."

"She's nice."

Nate smiled. "And the best cook in this part of Chicago, too."

"Her chocolate cake is just about the best thing that ever happened to me," Ryan agreed.

The wind shifted, and Nate noticed a muted clanging. "Hey," he said, turning. "You hear that?"

A moment later, Nate could see a fire engine coming up Clinton, the horses at full gallop, its bell sounding the alarm. As the team turned onto a side street—either Polk or Mather, he was pretty sure— he caught a glimpse of the steamer with its shining upright boiler.

Ryan faced him. "There must be a fire somewhere down there. Let's go look. I bet we could get there before the rest of the crowd—"

"It's probably just some coals from last night's fire. They'll have it out before we even get there."

"Not in this wind they won't."

Nate frowned. "I can't stay out too long."

Ryan walked sideways, peering into Nate's face. "It's hard for me to get out like this, Nate. I'm going to catch holy heck for it, so I'm at least going to do something exciting." When Nate didn't answer, Ryan frowned and turned away. Abruptly, he took off running down the boardwalk, his shoes pounding a hollow rhythm on the planks.

The wind scoured the boardwalk, swirling dust and bits of paper. Nate was sure Ryan would stop and wait for him. But he didn't.

"Ryan!" Nate shouted. Ryan didn't even pause. Angry, Nate started after him. It was stupid to get separated, especially at night. Whenever there were fires, there were people who crossed the bridges, coming out of Conley's Patch and looking for an opportunity to loot burning stores and homes.

Nate saw Ryan skidding as he turned the corner

onto Polk Street. Nate sprinted, trying to keep him in sight. At the corner of Canal Street, Ryan turned right, jumping off the boardwalk onto the street planks, then back up on the other side. He was still running hard. A few blocks down, a heavy wagon rumbled around the corner from De Koven Street, the driver whipping the team.

"Ryan!" Nate yelled. But if Ryan heard him, he didn't react. He kept going, slowing enough to look down Taylor Street as he crossed the intersection.

"This way, Nate!" he called, waving one hand over his head. Then he spun and ran up Taylor. As Nate followed, he could hear shouting.

After a moment, one word separated itself from the barrage of voices: "Fire!"

Julie closed the door, then stood just inside it, watching Mr. Black light his pipe. He glanced up at her, then down at the lucifer match he held tightly between his thumb and forefinger. His eyes squeezed nearly shut, he puffed at the pipe. Then he blew several smoke rings into the air. "You know your way around, Julie. Just make yourself comfortable. You may look at any book you like."

At that moment, Julie heard a wagon clattering past outside, the horses galloping hard. She looked out the front windows, but caught only a blur of motion. As the hoofbeats faded, she heard a man shout.

Mr. Black looked up. "That's probably a young fellow who works down at the Empire Slip unloading ships' cargo. We have all gotten used to him and his recklessness."

Julie nodded and pulled off her gloves, then slipped out of her cloak, laying it over the back of a reading bench. Her hair was windblown, and she combed it with her fingers, feeling almost grown up. Here she was, looking at books by herself, halfway across the city from her parents' town house.

She turned in a slow circle, trying to decide where to start. The books always looked magical to her. She loved opening the heavy leather covers, the sharp scent of the crisp new pages. The gold-lettered titles shone in the light from the gas lamps.

Mr. Black settled deeper into his chair behind the cash box. He puffed at his pipe, and soon Julie heard the scratching of his pen. She walked along the shelves, scanning the spines of the books. There were grand adventures, love stories, all of Shakespeare's plays, and the heavy, scholarly books Mr. Black collected. She glanced at him. "Excuse me?"

He looked up. "Yes?"

"Do you have Mr. Verne's new novel?"

"Over here, Julie," Mr. Black said. He scraped back his chair and stood, crossing the shop. He reached to pull a book from the shelf. "Mr. Verne has come up with another incredible tale. This one is as fanciful as *Journey to the Center of the Earth*."

Julie took the book from him. He was smiling. "Thank you," she said politely. "I can barely wait to read it. Father said he would buy it for me."

Mr. Black nodded. "Read a bit and see if you like it first."

Julie thanked him and started toward one of the pillowed benches along the far wall, but Mr. Black began talking and she turned to face him.

"It is no accident that Verne is a Frenchman," Mr. Black was saying. "English authors never would have conceived these ideas. They are too bound to worldly reality, as are most Americans now. We, of course, have such a tiny, short history as a nation that we—" Mr. Black stopped abruptly.

At that instant, Julie heard the hoofbeats of galloping horses again, and a clamoring bell. She turned to face the big windows at the front of the shop. Mr. Black was a half step ahead of her. He opened the door and went out. "It's a steamer." His voice was tight.

Julie felt her stomach clench as the fire engine clattered past. The shining boiler stood upright on its four-wheeled carriage. It chuffed out clouds of steam and cinders as the driver whipped the horses faster. Julie could just read the name painted on its side—LITTLE GIANT. Once it had gone by there was a faint glitter of still-glowing clinkers from its coal box scattered on the boards that covered the street.

"Is there another fire?" Julie took one hesitant step onto the boardwalk, and Mr. Black caught her arm.

"Go back inside, Julie."

She nodded, but didn't move, struggling to see up the dimly lit street. There was an unsettling orange cast to the night sky, and she could smell smoke. Her heart pounded in her chest. "Where is it? It's close, isn't it?"

Mr. Black pulled her gently. "Please go in, Julie. I'll find out where the fire is."

Julie stepped back into the doorway, watching

him go. Then, uneasy, she glanced up and down the boardwalk. No one else was near. She slipped back out, moving away from the door far enough to see up the street.

The fire engine was stopped at the corner next to a high-wheeled cart hung with hoses. As Julie watched, a fireman from the Little Giant pulled one hose from the fireplug and attached another. A burly man was laying out lengths of hose on the other side of the engine. She could see the brass fittings gleaming in the odd, reddish light.

Mr. Black ran to the corner. Julie saw him stop beneath the streetlamp, shouting something to the firemen, but none of them turned to answer him. They were too intent on their work.

Once the hoses were run from the fireplug on the corner to one side of the steamer engine, the men attached even longer sections of hose to the other side. Then they started their pump. With the steam-driven pump forcing the water, the stream from the hose was powerful enough to reach to the roofs of the two-story buildings where Taylor Street crossed Jefferson.

Julie heard another steamer bell clanging somewhere close by. Shouts rang out, then she heard a woman screaming. A cow, bawling in pain, seemed to come out of nowhere, galloping down the boardwalk. Her halter was loose, and a lead rope trailed out behind her.

Julie jumped backward, letting the panicked animal go past, then stepped cautiously onto the boardwalk again. She looked toward the corner, her heart thudding against her ribs. Mr. Black was nowhere to be seen. She was alone.

Chapter Five

The streetlamps cast their amber glow into the smoky air. Nate turned the corner onto Taylor. A block or two up the street, he saw an ominous halo of flickering light. It framed the buildings on the south side. The wind was unnaturally warm, and there was an odd, sharp scent of smoke and blistering varnish in the air.

There were firemen on the corner, scrambling to set up their pump engine, the hoses already strung from the fireplug. The stoker was pitching lumps of coal into the steam engine. Another fireman was standing off to one side, arguing with a man wearing a well-cut waistcoat and trousers. There was a hose cart, too, its spool turning slowly as the driver's assistant dragged out the hoses.

Nate slowed, trying to see Ryan. People were coming out of their houses all along Taylor Street. Nate heard a woman screaming, her voice rising above the growing din. Hoofbeats behind him made Nate turn. A wagon loaded with wooden crates started up Taylor Street, then stopped when the driver saw the fire. He whipped the horses around, nearly upsetting the wagon as he turned back.

There was a girl standing on the boardwalk. Her dress was obviously expensive, flounced and ruffled. Nate wondered for an instant what she was doing there this time of evening. There was no carriage waiting.

Turning, he caught a glimpse of Ryan, dancing from one foot to the other, shouting at one of the firemen. The man made an angry gesture that was easy to understand even at this distance. He wanted Ryan to get out of his way.

Nate swore under his breath. This was just like Ryan—running up to a fireman like a little kid. Nate watched Ryan run across the street, then hesitate as if he were trying to decide which way to go next. He suddenly veered again, running up Taylor, straight toward the ominous glow that rose from the next block. Nate ran after him, then, with a sudden shock of recognition, realized where he was. The O'Learys' place was less than a block away on De Koven Street. Was their house on fire now?

Nate tried to keep Ryan in sight, but it was hard. People were streaming into the streets from every doorway, some of them dressed in their nightclothes, all of them trying to see where the fire was.

Nate walked as fast as he could, rising onto his tiptoes to try to see over the crowds that clogged the intersection with Jefferson Street. When he couldn't, he worked his way to the edge of the throng. Climbing up onto a porch, he spotted another steam engine setting up at the fireplug on the corner of Des Plaines Street—just one block ahead.

The firemen were running back and forth to the plug, shouting and gesturing as they hooked up the first of their hoses. One man had led the team of horses a little way off to get them away from the heat. As Nate watched, the firemen stoked their steam engine with more coal and turned on the pump. The stream of water arced upward from the hose. Three men dragged it forward, the first of them aiming the water high.

Nate watched as the firemen disappeared behind the corner of a building. The wind-whipped smoke darkened a little as the water hit the roof. Nate shook his head. The steam engines were remarkable. The firemen would probably be able to control this fire in an hour or so. Still, Ryan had been right. It was going to be quite a show.

Nate turned a slow circle, looking for Ryan. Maybe he'd gone up De Koven to see if the O'Learys' place was on fire? Unsure of what else to do, Nate started down Taylor Street again. The hoses stretched across a vacant lot, and he could see flames shooting from the roofs of two old wooden barns that stood close together.

As he walked, the heat increased until he had to stop, blinking and shielding his face with one hand. He still couldn't see the O'Leary cottage—but it looked like the McLaughlins' house was afire.

"Get out of here, kid!"

Nate spun around at the angry growl. A man in a belted rubber coat was glaring down at him. He wore the standard leather fireman's helmet, except for the lettering blazoned across its peak. Nate blinked in the smoky air, trying to read it. The letters suddenly leaped into place when the fireman turned to face the streetlamp—CHIEF FIRE MARSHAL. Nate swallowed nervously. This was Marshal Williams, the man in charge of every fire department in Chicago—the man Mr. Oliver had talked about a hundred times.

"Do you live up there?"

Nate shook his head.

"Then move along. People like you make it harder for us to fight the fires."

Nate pointed up Taylor Street. "I have a friend up there somewhere, and he—"

"I advise you to clear out, son," Marshal Williams said. "If your friend is in trouble, we'll do our best to get him out." He stepped around Nate and ran on toward the steamer, shouting orders at the firemen.

Nate stared. He could see flames now, sparkling in the night. The heat on his face was uncomfortable, and he wanted nothing more than to follow Marshal Williams's advice. But what if something happened to Ryan? How could he ever explain it to Ryan's parents? Or to Aunt Ruth? She would never forgive him for being a coward if Ryan needed his help.

Nate stared at the people who came toward him, fleeing the flames. Two women walked together, their hair burned close to their scalps. They were both wearing nightclothes, walking hand in hand, their faces blank. A man behind them was carrying a box of silver plate, engraved serving trays jutting up at odd angles. He had wild eyes, as though he was about to start screaming. A woman pulling two small children in a play cart walked behind him. They were both crying, rubbing at their stinging eyes.

The wind buffeted Nate, raising a fountain of cinders. A woman near him shrieked, slapping at her apron. Nate blinked, knowing he should follow the crowd, should get away from the fire, go home. But how could he leave Ryan?

Over the noise of the crowd milling around him, Nate heard another alarm, this time to the north. Maybe the fire had spread to another block. He surveyed the scene, balling his fists in anger. Where was Ryan?

"Hey, you! Boy!"

Someone grabbed at Nate's arm. Startled, he jerked free, turning to see a dapper gentleman staring intently at him. "Can I hire you?"

A heavyset woman elbowed Nate to one side. He stepped back to let her pass.

"Do you want a job?" the man demanded, almost shouting. "I own the bookstore, just over there." He pointed.

Nate hesitated, glancing around once more, hoping to see Ryan's face among the throng of strangers.

"Are you looking for someone? Do you have family near here?" The man's face was intense, his eyes narrowed against the acrid wind.

Nate shook his head. "I can't find my friend."

"He probably ran home. Now, do you want a job or not? I have to find somebody fast. This fire looks like it might spread before they get it under control."

Nate scanned the crowd. Maybe Ryan *had* gotten scared and gone home. After all, he had never seen a big fire up close like this. Nate looked at the man. He was still waiting, glaring.

"I'll pay well. All you have to do is help me load books into my wagon. Then you can be on your way."

Nate nodded. The man was probably right. And Ryan wasn't foolish enough to walk straight into the fire. Aunt Ruth might even forgive him for sneaking out if he brought home a little extra money.

"This way, then," the man said, pushing his way through the crowd.

Nate did his best to keep up as the man ran back along Taylor Street. As they neared the little bookstore, Nate saw the girl he had noticed before. She was still standing on the boardwalk, her face pale, her hands clasped.

"Mr. Black! Are you all right?" she called.

"I'll have you out of here in no time, Julie," he answered as they got closer. "This boy is going to help us load the wagon."

The man slowed his step enough to escort the girl back inside. Then he gestured for Nate to follow him through the shop and out the back door into the alleyway. There was a wagon, the team tied to a hitching rail. Both horses were wild-eyed, fidgeting in the harness, their manes blowing in the wind. Nate looked up the alleyway, then down it. It ended less than a block east of where he was standing, at a tall wooden fence that had been built straight across it.

Mr. Black pointed at the rig. "We'll load my collection first, then as much of the other inventory as we can." Without another word, he went back inside. Nate saw the girl standing in the doorway. She stared at him. She looked scared.

Nate studied the buildings across the alley. They were silhouetted against the weird orange glow of the sky. He turned into the wind, squinting. At the other end of the block, the wooden roof of a livery stable was smoking. He could hear the horses squealing in fear. Mr. Black's team answered, stamping their hooves and shifting nervously in their harness.

Nate made a sudden decision and ran down the alley. Black silt underfoot made a strange scraping sound as he ran. There was a wide door at the rear of the stables. Nate lifted the bar and swung it wide. Smoke billowed out, and after a moment, Nate could see inside.

Every stall had one or two horses in it, frantic, kicking at the rails. Where were the livery men? Ryan's father would never leave animals to die like this. Running, coughing in the thick smoke, Nate went from one stall gate to the next, flinging them wide.

Some of the horses plunged through the open gates immediately, heading for the wide doors at a panicked gallop. Others were afraid to move until Nate slapped their rumps, startling them into action. Luckily, none of them balked, and within seconds

Nate was out in the alley again, choking and gasping for fresher air. He watched the last three horses gallop to the end of the alley and plunge to a halt, whinnying at the confusion in the street.

Nate turned back toward the bookstore, glad to have set the animals free. Some of the horses would probably die in the fire, anyway, but at least now they had a chance.

Chapter Six

Heart pounding, Julie followed Mr. Black into the shop. The air was so smoky that it stung her eyes and burned her lungs. All she wanted in the whole world was for her father to drive up Taylor Street, lashing the horses into a gallop as he came to get her.

"Julie?" Mr. Black was sweating, his face flushed. "Where's the boy?"

"I don't know," Julie answered. She turned to look toward the back door just as the boy was coming inside.

"Come in, boy," Mr. Black said. "I need your help."

"My name is Nate."

Mr. Black was already pointing at the shelves that held his collection of fine old books. "I want to start with these, Nate. All the dark leather bindings on the top two shelves. Once you finish, we'll load those." He indicated the gold-embossed volumes of Shakespeare's works. Julie stared at him. His gestures were awkward, stiff. His voice was rough, grating.

He was terrified, she realized. But if he was that afraid, why were they staying? Why couldn't they just get in the wagon and leave now?

"Have you got crates or boxes I can put them in?" Nate asked.

Julie watched Mr. Black's face. For a second, it was blank, as though he hadn't understood the question. Then he strode to the back of the shop, jerking open the storeroom door. "In here."

Nate went past Julie, shooting a glance over his shoulder. "Will you help me?"

Julie nodded hesitantly and followed him. Maybe Mr. Black would leave once his rare books were safely in the wagon.

"I'll pay you a day's wages for an hour's work, Nate," Mr. Black was saying. "But you're going to have to work *hard*."

"Yes, sir," Nate said evenly as Mr. Black came out of the storeroom, hurrying past them.

Nate disappeared and came back a second later, carrying two crates. "Can you take these?".

Julie reached out, then stared at him for a moment, holding the rough wood gingerly away from her dress. He went back into the storeroom and emerged with four crates stacked in his arms. In seconds, he was loading them with books.

Julie stood still, watching Nate work. Mr. Black was stacking his account books. He glanced up. "Please help, Julie. The books are very valuable."

Awkward, holding the crates almost at arm's length, Julie made her way to the front of the shop. She set them down near Nate.

He glanced at her. "I'm taller. I'll keep pulling the books off the top shelves. This isn't going to take very long. You can start down there."

Julie hesitated, looking toward the door again. The air was sharp with smoke.

"You expecting someone to come?" Nate asked.

She nodded. "My father."

Nate took down ten or fifteen books, placing them in the crate. "Does he know where you are?"

Julie blinked back tears.

"Don't worry," Nate said. "We'll be all right."

"Load each crate as soon as you have it filled." Mr. Black almost had to shout over the street noise now.

Nate looked at her. "Can you carry these once they're full?"

Julie bent and tried to lift the heavy crate. She managed to straighten up, then stood, swaying for a few seconds before she had to put it down.

"If you could drag them as far as the back door, it would help," Nate told her.

Julie gripped the topmost slat and walked backward, taking tiny steps. The front of her skirt dragged the floor, and she had to be careful to keep it clear. She managed to drag the books to the back door and stood straight again, peering out.

The buildings weren't afire yet, but the alley was filling with people and the air was hazy with smoke. Everyone seemed to be intent on getting out. Mr. Black had talked to the firemen. Maybe they had told him it was safe to stay long enough to load his books. Julie wiped at a trickle of sweat at her temple, then ducked inside. She carried empty crates on her way back.

Nate looked up. "Thanks."

Julie met his eyes for a second. "It's getting hotter

in the alley." Her voice sounded odd in her own ears, small and frightened.

"Could you see flames?"

Julie shook her head. "Not yet."

Nate gestured toward the front. "Go see if it's moved any closer from that direction."

Julie nodded and went to the door. As she looked out, the wind whipped her skirt against her legs, making the woolen stockings itch even more. The street was choked with people now. Wagons, jammed with piles of their belongings, stood end-to-end from the corner all the way past the shop and down to Canal Street.

Julie stared. Men, women, and crying children weaved in and out of the wagons, carrying bundles of clothing, stacks of papers, chairs, lamps, anything they could manage. One woman balanced a wailing baby and a struggling newborn calf in her arms.

As Julie watched, amazed, two loose horses plunged through the crowd, knocking one old woman onto the boardwalk. A man helped her to her feet, and they stumbled on together.

"How close is it?" Nate yelled.

Startled, Julie turned to face him. "I can't tell.

There are so many people. I don't see flames."

"Keep working, Nate!" Julie heard Mr. Black shout. He was hoisting a full crate to his shoulder, hurrying toward the alley door.

Nate glanced after Mr. Black, then came to stand beside Julie. He whistled between his teeth. "We need to get going or we'll be trapped."

Julie could feel herself trembling. "But what if my father comes."

Nate shrugged. "How? Can he fly over these crowds?"

Julie shook her head angrily, but before she could answer, Mr. Black shouted again. "Come on, you two. We haven't got time to waste!"

Julie faced him. "The street is too crowded. You'll never even get the wagon out of here."

Mr. Black shook his head. "But I have to get the books—"

"She's right," Nate cut him off. "We should leave."

Mr. Black stepped back, pulling out his wallet. "Thank you for the help, then." He pulled out five dollars and handed it to Nate. His eyes flickered around the shop. "Just help me load a few more. Then you can be on your way, and I'll take Julie home."

Julie watched Nate pocket the bill, a frown on his face. He stepped out onto the crowded boardwalk, looking up the street, toward the fire. Julie edged out into the wind, straining to see through the thick crowds and the haze. "What are you going to do?" She pulled her hair back and held it out of her face.

Nate spoke without looking at her. "I'm going to load three or four more of his stupid crates, then I'm leaving. This whole block is going up."

Julie looked nervously back through the doorway. Mr. Black was working frantically. She called out to him, but he didn't answer or even pause to look at her. He had started on another shelf of books.

She glanced at Nate and was startled at how pale his face was. He pointed. "I can see the flames."

Julie stood on her tiptoes and caught her breath. Across the street, at the end of the block, flames were darting in and out of the smoke like glowing snakes.

Nate gestured at Julie, and she followed him back inside. Working like a demon, he emptied two shelves' worth of books. Julie helped, straightening the volumes so that more could fit, dragging the full crates out.

"I'll load these," Nate announced. "Then I'll be on my way."

Mr. Black nodded vaguely, without looking up. His face was flushed, and he was muttering to himself. Nate shot Julie a look, hoping she wouldn't insist on staying. He was relieved when she turned to come with him.

The hot wind hit Nate the second he stepped into the alley. There was a stunning jumble of noise in the air: voices, screams, and the cries of terror-stricken animals. He set the books in the wagon, then turned to look at Julie. "Let's go. Right now. Before he notices."

Julie was shaking her head, blinking back tears. "We can't just leave him. You saw how close the fire is."

Nate stared at her, astonished. "So did he. And, somehow, those books are more important to him than his own life. He's crazy."

Julie knotted her hands together. "No, he isn't," she argued. "My father says that Mr. Black is the smartest man he knows."

"Not tonight he isn't." Nate watched anger darken her face. The smell of smoke was sharp, painful. He knew the fire could burst out around them at any second, cutting off any chance of escape. He had heard enough of Mr. Oliver's stories to know that flames traveled faster than anyone ever thought they could—especially in a wind like this. He thought about Ryan and said a silent prayer for his friend. "We have to leave now," he said aloud.

Julie backed toward the door. "I'll go get Mr. Black. He can come with us."

Nate shook his head, but she was already gone. He could hear her voice at first, then the hubbub in the alleyway drowned it out. He fought with himself. He knew it was foolish to stay a second longer, but he couldn't just leave Julie. He slammed the heel of his hand into the wagon gate, then turned and went back inside.

Mr. Black was standing with his arms full of books. Julie was tugging at him, pleading. Mr. Black looked up and focused on Nate. "Is the wagon loaded?"

Nate nodded. "Not quite, but almost. If we leave this minute, we just might make it out of here." Mr. Black's eyes were odd and glittery. He didn't answer. "Julie," Nate said quietly. "Let's go now."

Julie looked at him over her shoulder, and he

could see that she was crying. "He'll come. Just let me talk to him for a minute more."

"We don't have that long," Nate said flatly. "Mr. Black?"

Without answering, Mr. Black went back to the bookshelves. Nate reached out and took Julie's hand. Startled, she spun around, and he pulled her toward the front door. Mr. Black didn't even look up as they went out onto the boardwalk.

The instant they came out into the wind, Nate saw the flames almost directly across the street. He glanced upward, looking at the front of the bookstore. High above his head, the planks were starting to smoke.

Chapter Seven

Julie wrenched free from Nate's grip on her fore-arm as he pulled her outside. "We can't just leave Mr. Black—"

"There's nothing we can do." Nate jabbed an index finger toward the two-story building just across the street. "It's too late. *Look*."

Julie stared, her throat tight with fear. The wood was literally smoking. It was about to burst into flames.

"Are you coming with me or not?" Nate was glar-ing at her.

Julie glanced up the crowded street, then leaned back through the door. "Mr. Black?" She screamed his name, but he did not answer. Julie's knees were trembling. "Please," she shouted. "Come with us!"

"You can't change his mind," Nate was saying.

Julie looked up at the smoking roofline once more, then back at Nate. A scream in the street made her whirl around. A woman, dressed only in her night-clothes, was pointing at a fresh outbreak of flames two buildings down.

Nate led the way into the street. Julie gathered her skirts in one hand and stepped off the boardwalk, fol-lowing him. They threaded their way between two wagons, the horses sweating with fear and pawing at the street planks. Julie saw a little boy pushed down, sprawling on the rough wood, and she gasped. An instant later his half-dressed mother pulled him back onto his feet, and they disappeared into the crowd.

Half a block on, Julie managed to glance back at the bookstore. The roof was in flames. She stumbled, wrenching free. "Mr. Black!" she whispered.

Nate gently turned her around. "You can't help him. No one can."

Julie watched for another few seconds as dark smoke rolled out of the open doorway. Was he still in there, trying to pack his precious books? Julie saw a sudden gush of smoke burst from the windows as they shattered, then cascaded into glittering piles of glass. The whole building was suddenly flickering with flames.

Julie pressed her hand against her mouth, fighting a strangling sense of panic. She felt Nate's hand tighten on her own, pulling her to one side, out of the way of a passing wagon. She glanced back at the bookstore, now a mass of flame, then turned and started walking again, unable to speak.

Still holding her hand, Nate steadied her as the crowd shifted and eddied around them. The human crush was almost more than she could bear. A burly man who stank of whiskey said something to her, leaning close, but she could make no sense of his words. An elderly woman, lying flat on a door carried by three other women, smiled weakly at Julie as they passed. A young woman shrieked and screamed over and over, repeating a name. Her husband? One of her children?

"You can come with me to my aunt's boarding-house," Nate was shouting, close to her ear. "We'll be safe there."

Julie nodded, only half understanding what he was saying. She could not stop glancing at the inferno behind them. A little boy darted in front of Nate, then went on, nearly running beneath a wagon. The driver cursed, shaking his fist.

Julie's eyes stung, and she wiped the sweat from her forehead. It was as though the whole world had become hellish, engulfed in fire. She half turned for a last glance up Taylor Street. The bookstore was hidden behind a sheet of flame.

"Follow me," Nate shouted into her ear. "Stay close."

Julie nodded, but when he let go of her arm, she stumbled. Hoisting her skirts in both hands, she ran a few steps to catch up, afraid to be alone in the terrified, chaotic crowd. Julie felt the hundreds of people around her like a pressing weight as they neared Canal Street. It was hard to breathe. The air was sooty and hot.

A woman on Julie's right pressed so close that Julie could feel the buttons that ran down the side of her dress. Her bustle was askew, sagging, her train torn and filthy. Ahead of them, Julie saw one man throwing punches at another. They seemed to sink into the crowd like stones into water, and disappeared.

"This way!" Nate yelled, jutting his chin to show her the direction he meant. Julie nodded so he would know she had understood him. They began to angle across the street, maneuvering through the throng. An old man shook his fist at Julie, and she apologized for bumping him, but his attention was already elsewhere. He carried a little dog in his arms, and it growled and snapped as she made her way past him.

The crowd spewed out of Taylor Street into the intersection with Canal. Suddenly there was a little more room, a little less crush. Julie pulled in a deep breath of hot smoky air and coughed.

"Are you all right?" Nate's flushed face was close, and Julie realized that they could walk side by side here.

"Yes," she told him, looking back over her shoulder. The sea of flames behind them was rapidly engulfing this end of Taylor Street, driven by the wind. Julie's dress fluttered up around her ankles, and she fought to keep it modestly in place.

"Where do you live?"

Julie pointed. "Across the river, in the South Division." She watched an odd expression pass across his features and wondered what he was thinking.

"Aunt Ruth's boardinghouse is a lot closer. I want to go there first." Abruptly, he lurched to one side, slapping at his own shirt.

At first, Julie couldn't tell why he had done it. Then she realized he was looking down at his feet. She followed his gaze. There on the pavement, just in front of him, lay half a shingle, still burning along one edge. As she watched, the wind scooted it along the planks, then let it lie still again. When Nate looked back at her, Julie was astonished at how pale his flushed face had become.

"It fell out of the sky," he said quietly, looking back down Canal Street toward Taylor. "That's nearly a block. The wind carried it this far."

Julie nodded, understanding. Maybe the firemen wouldn't be able to put the fire out this time. If it could jump whole blocks, how could they? Maybe nothing was going to stop it.

She thought about her father and clenched her fists. He would look for her, if he could. When he saw the burned rubble that had been the bookshop, he was going to think she was dead. Julie imagined her mother, stricken with grief, her father trying not to weep. She had to find him somehow—or make sure that he could find her.

Nate kicked at the burning shingle, then looked up, scanning Canal Street. As far as he could see there were no flames ahead of them—yet. The wind gusted, and Nate saw Julie reach up to capture her hair. The crowds around them had slowed a little, and he saw a few people standing still, their faces grim. Some of them probably had lost their homes and had nowhere to go.

"My father will come looking for me," Julie said suddenly. She kept glancing back toward Taylor Street. "Maybe I shouldn't go too much farther."

Nate fought an impulse to leave her there, if that was what she wanted. But he knew he couldn't. It was obvious that she would have no idea how to take care of herself in this crowd. "You can't stay this close to the fire," he said aloud.

Julie ducked her head. "I don't know what to do."

Nate shrugged. "You can come with me. My aunt Ruth and Mr. Oliver will know what you should do."

"Mr. Oliver?" She looked confused.

"He's a fireman; one of our boarders."

Julie hesitated, then nodded. He was relieved when she started forward.

The crowds were thinner on Canal Street and they could walk much faster. People were spreading out, and the wagons were able to make their way through the teeming traffic.

Julie gathered her skirts and tried hard to keep up. Nate kept glancing at her sidelong. It was obvious from her expensive silk dress that she was the daughter of a wealthy man. She looked out of place walking through the dirty streets with the crowds. People like her were usually the ones helping, the ones ladling out soup or dropping off old clothes for the needy.

"Oh, no! God, no!"

The man's voice came from behind them. Nate spun and looked at him. He was pointing over the rooftops. Nate followed his gesture and saw smoke rising from the barely visible steeple of St. Paul's Catholic Church.

"St. Paul's is on fire," Julie said in a low, disbelieving voice. "Where are the firemen? Why doesn't someone put it out?"

Nate shrugged, hoping she didn't expect him to

answer. The way Mr. Oliver had looked at supper, it was hard to imagine the exhausted firemen being able to fight any part of this fire.

"I was christened in that church," Julie said softly. "My father took groceries there this afternoon for the refugees from last night's fire. We attend Mass there sometimes."

A rush of heavy footsteps made Nate turn. Seven or eight men were sprinting up Canal Street. They carried bulging feed sacks over their shoulders. There was something different about them, and it took Nate a few seconds to realize what it was.

These men were fully dressed, and their clothes were clean. The fire had not driven them from their homes into soot-filled streets. They had come from an area untouched by the fire—and they had come to steal. They weren't carrying their most treasured possessions. They were making off with someone else's.

"Make way!" the man in the lead shouted out.

Nate moved to one side. He tried to pull Julie with him, but she shook him off, glancing backward at the men as they got closer. One of them passed so close that he brushed against her, knocking her off balance. Nate reached to help her, but she shook her head. Once she had recovered and settled back into a striding pace, she looked indignantly at him.

"Were those men looters? Where are the police?"

Nate shook his head. "They have more than enough to do tonight, Julie."

As they walked on, she stared at him and he waited for her to say more, but she did not. Suddenly, he felt a sharp pain on his forehead. Instinctively, he slapped at it, as though it were a mosquito. His hand came away smudged with black. He looked up into the sky. The wind was shifting, confettied with tiny embers and fragments of black and white ash. Beside him, Julie was brushing at her skirts, tilting her head back to watch the ashes fall.

"Keep shaking out your skirt," Nate told her. "And be careful of your hair." He slapped at a stinging pin-prick on the back of his neck.

Julie didn't answer him as they stepped off the boardwalk at the corner of Mather Street. She was looking at the church as they crossed. "St. Paul's is really on fire," she said in a low voice.

Before he could stop her, she had turned up Mather, joining a ragged parade of spectators walking toward the church. Nate hesitated, looking wistfully into the night, northward toward home, then reluctantly started after her. "Julie?" He hurried to catch up. "Julie, where are you going?"

"Look," she said, her eyes fixed on the steeple high atop St. Paul's.

Nate uneasily gauged the distance back to the wall of glowing orange flames. It was creeping closer. He was pretty sure that Ewing Street was on fire now. That meant the wind had carried the blaze almost four blocks.

Nate turned and looked across the street. He stared at Bateham's Mill, seeing the twenty-five-foot stacks of kindling and the piles of furniture lumber as if for the first time. It would only take one ember and this steady wind to turn the whole place into a torch.

Chapter Eight

Julie couldn't believe St. Paul's was burning. Surely God would not allow it to be destroyed? But the flames were clinging to the cupola below the steeple, flattened against the wood by the wind. As she got closer, she could see that someone had rigged a long ramp up to the wide front doors that slanted at a gentler angle than the steps. Firemen were filing in and out in an uneven line. They were carrying out holy relics. Three men were staggering beneath the weight of the font. Others carried parts of the elaborate altar and carved wooden crucifixes.

One fireman, carrying a large statue of a saint on his back, paused at the end of the ramp, shouting out a question Julie couldn't hear. Whatever it was, it made his companions laugh. But the laughter lasted only a few seconds. Then the flames on the cupola leaped upward along the side of the steeple, doubling in size as the wind gusted.

As Julie reached the raised boardwalk in front of the church, she saw a hook and ladder wagon pulled by two bay horses rumble around the corner. As the wagoner pulled the team to a halt, Julie could read the name PROTECTION emblazoned on the side of the wagon. The firemen rushed to set up a long ladder against the side of St. Paul's.

Julie heard shouting and turned back toward Canal Street. She spotted Nate. He was glaring at her through the crowd. Just beyond, she saw several men waving their arms over their heads, flagging down a steamer. It slowed a little as the crowd surged, people trying to get out of its way. The driver pulled the horses in a long arc onto Mather Street, and Julie could read the name as it rolled closer— JACOB REHM.

The team's hooves clattered on the raised plank roadway. Within minutes, a fireman on a ladder was dousing the flames. Julie exhaled in relief as the blaze was put out. St. Paul's was saved. The crowd began to cheer.

"Julie!"

Nate was shouting from behind her again. She glanced at him but refused to turn around. She didn't know what to do. Nate had been kind to her and he seemed trustworthy. But maybe it was foolish to go back into the crush of the crowds. It would be easier for her father to find her here, and this was the logical place for him to look. Once the fire was under control, St. Paul's would be helping the refugees.

A man near Julie whooped as the fireman came down the ladder, grinning at the crowd. Then the cheers turned to shouts of warning. The fire had rekindled itself on the roof. Julie caught her breath as the fireman went back up the ladder. This time, he held the stream of water on the flames until they had been completely drowned.

Once he was back on the ground, the man from the Protection pulled the ladder down. It slewed sideways, falling so hard that it broke. Julie squinted, staring at the roof. There were no flames.

Nate appeared alongside her and caught her hand.

"What are you doing? We shouldn't stay here."

Julie pulled free, startled and angry. She did not want to leave yet. She felt safer here. There were two policemen walking along the edge of the board-walk. She could see a priest talking to a family near the rectory. The crowd seemed calmer around the church. The idea of going back to Canal Street and being pushed along by terrified strangers made her shiver, in spite of the hot wind.

Julie faced Nate, making a sudden decision. "Thank you for your help, but I'm going to stay. Maybe I'll ask one of the policemen to take me home." She said it as calmly as she could. Just saying it made her feel better, less frightened. It was dangerous walking with Nate on the dark, crowded streets.

Nate shook his head. "Those policemen don't have time for you right now."

Julie straightened her skirts and raised her head high. Without a word, she walked away from him. He would see. She would tell the policemen who her father was, and they would find some way to take her home.

The officers had worked their way along the Mather boardwalk, past the old-fashioned house on the corner. Julie ran to catch up with them, the smoky air rasping at her throat. "Excuse me?"

Neither of them turned to look at her; they were absorbed in their own conversation. One was heavyset and bald. He was gesturing emphatically. "It could jump the river. How can you say it won't?"

The other policeman shook his head. "They'll keep it from coming much farther north, and it can't spread much farther eastward. It'll have to stop when it hits last night's burn. There's nothing left up there but sixteen acres of ash and dirt."

"Excuse me, please?" Julie repeated, raising her voice.

The heavyset man turned, scowling. "What? What do you want?"

"I'm Julie Flynn. I need help getting home," she began. She could hear the strain in her own voice. She felt like she was about to cry.

"Where do you live?"

She had expected kindness from the policeman; it was not there. "My father—"

"I asked where you live." He was frowning at her, impatient.

"On Michigan," Julie told him. "On the lake."

"You'd best get back there, then," the second policeman interjected tersely. He didn't even look at her as he spoke.

"Where are your parents?" the heavyset man demanded.

Julie shook her head, stunned by the annoyance in his voice.

"Find someone you can trust, little girl, and go home. Tell your father to get his family as far north and west as he can tonight." The policeman said it curtly, then they both stepped around her, resuming their conversation.

Julie watched them talk to a fireman for a few seconds. Then all three of them helped the crew of the Jacob Rehm push the crowd back so the steamer could be moved closer to the church.

"See? I told you." She turned to see Nate coming toward her. He pointed across the street. "Those lumberyards are going to burn like pitch in a bonfire, and the firemen aren't going to be able to do anything about it."

Julie bristled. "My father says the firemen in Chicago are the finest professionals in the country."

Nate laughed. "One of our boarders is a fireman. He

says it's the weariest force in the country. And he told me they have frayed hoses and worn-out steamers."

Julie looked past him, fighting tears. She wanted to believe she would be safe here, close to St. Paul's. She was tired of being afraid, of running.

"The roof! The roof's on fire again!" someone shouted. There was an instant of silence, then people began to call out to the firemen rewinding the Jacob Rehm's hoses. The men whirled and ran back, aiming a stream of water as high as they could without a ladder—but it was no use this time. The flames were on the east end of the roof, burning backward against the wind.

"The mill's afire!" a woman screamed.

Julie whirled around to face the enormous stacks of thin, dry kindling. A flash of light caught her eye and she looked up. Red-hot fragments of what looked like roof shingles were sailing overhead, streaking like Chinese rockets against the night sky. The ugly truth was too obvious to ignore. Each and every one of them could start another fire.

Nate leaned close so that she could hear him above the din. "It's dangerous here, and I'm getting out. If you want to come with me, you can."

Julie glanced at him, then looked back at the church just as the roof fell in on itself, sending a shower of sparks skyward. A woman standing just in front of them collapsed. Her husband bent over her on the boardwalk, calling her name.

"Julie?" Nate had already taken a few steps. "Are you coming?" He spoke over his shoulder.

She nodded. What else could she do?

Nate walked fast, worried about Aunt Ruth, wondering how long it had been since he'd left the boardinghouse. There was no fire to the north that he could see—she was in no danger yet—but she would be frantic if she had discovered he was gone.

The crowds were thick. He had to keep turning every few seconds to make sure Julie was following. She walked so awkwardly in her full, elaborate dress that she had trouble keeping up. He had almost left her at the church. He was glad he hadn't. He already felt guilty about letting Ryan run off.

He pushed his way through a knot of people standing in the middle of Canal Street. They were facing the lumberyard, watching the flames spread over the stacks of kindling. The steamers were fighting that fire now. St. Paul's roof was nearly consumed, the flames a bright orange against the night sky.

"Wait for me!"

Nate stopped impatiently as Julie struggled to slip between two men who seemed not to notice that she was there at all. Their eyes were on the growing wall of flame that rose out of Bateham's Mill. Nate stood still until Julie got close to him. "Can't you keep up any better?"

"I'm trying," she said.

"You're going to have to try harder or we might not make it." Nate was about to go on when he saw her eyes flood with tears. He started to say something, but she silenced him with a gesture.

She wiped at her face, swallowing hard, then motioned for him to keep going. "I'll manage, thank you."

Nate glanced back down Mather Street. The mill yard was awash in flames. "We have to get out of here."

Julie nodded, then looked past him. Suddenly, her eyes went wide with fear. He spun around to see a team of horses bearing down on them, the pounding of their hooves dulled by the noise of the crowd. The driver was standing, one arm cocked over his head to crack the whip. The wagon was full of what looked like rags.

Nate pulled Julie to one side. As the wagon passed them, he could see over the side rails. People lay like cord wood, wrapped in sheets or a hodgepodge of clothing. He saw blood soaking through one man's bandages. Another man, next to him, had been badly burned. His skin was blistered, blotched red and white. Nate heard Julie make a small, frightened sound and saw her look aside.

Nate guided Julie forward, slowing his pace to hers, weaving through the mass of refugees. The sky above them was a nightmare of red and black as the wind increased. Boards and shingles began to fall, gigantic misshapen cinders that landed in the street, on people's heads and shoulders, setting fire to the wooden buildings that faced Canal Street.

A carriage horse reared ahead of them, squealing in fear. Nate saw a flaming board drop from the sky, landing half across its back. For a few seconds, Nate smelled, above all the other bitter odors of the fire, the ugly stench of burning horsehair. The poor animal hunched, rippling its skin, confused by the pain, then shied as the board slid to the street.

Julie tugged at Nate's hand, pointing off to the east. Nate saw a freight car stranded on the tracks that ran close to the river. Flames were pouring out of its doors. There was a man silhouetted against the fire. He was hopping from one foot to the other, a bizarre, disjointed movement. Was he on fire? It was impossible to tell from this distance. Nate turned away.

A sudden chorus of shouts made him draw Julie to one side again. This time, a steamer chuffed past, its team weary and sweat soaked, its men not much better off. As soon as it passed, a second engine turned onto Canal from West Harrison Street. People moved sideways, shoving to clear the road. A woman carrying a crate of clucking chickens bumped into Nate. He let go of Julie's hand, and she stumbled over a blackened board.

Nate grabbed at her arm to pull her upright, and she smiled apologetically, gathering her skirts in her free hand. For the first time, Nate noticed how dirty she had gotten. Her yellow plaid bodice was smudged with soot. Her hemline was black from dragging on the plank streets. She didn't look much like the prim rich girl he had seen standing in front of Mr. Black's bookstore.

Nate looked down at his own shirt. The white cotton was streaked black and brown. His shoes were scuffed and filthy with clinging ash. Aunt Ruth was not likely to forgive him for ruining his clothes—or for sneaking out tonight again. The best he could do to make amends was to get home quickly and safely.

The crowds had come to a stop. People were pushed together so tightly that no one could move. Nate half turned and looked back down Canal Street. Frantic citizens were emerging from the flame-ridden streets to the west, carrying bags and boxes piled high with their belongings. As he watched, many of them were setting down their loads in the center of the street, then turning to run off toward home again. Were they moving their households out onto Canal Street in hopes that the fire wouldn't get this far?

Nate squeezed his eyes shut, then opened them. The eerie red-orange light that flooded the city made everything look nightmarish, strange. The hot wind was constant, spreading the flames. The fire was on both sides of Canal Street now, and not more than three blocks behind them. Still, few people were running. Few people had the strength to run. Nate swallowed painfully. His throat was dry, and he was incredibly thirsty.

Nate tried to walk a little faster. Julie managed to keep up. He found himself staring at the planked street, thinking about the flaming cinders. How long would it be before the street itself was burning?

· They came to the intersection where Canal crossed Van Buren Street, and Nate looked sidelong at the bridge. The enormous supports, shaped like halved wagon wheels, were as yet unharmed. The bridge was full of people and wagons, and the traffic was moving at a good clip in both directions. It slowed only as pedestrians encountered the crush on Canal Street and tried to manuever around the piles of household goods, clothing, and furniture.

As Nate watched, a ticking-covered mattress was set on fire by a flying cinder. The wind fanned the flames, then lifted the edge of the mattress. A strong gust turned it over once, then twice, spattering sparks across the street planks. Twisting like a live thing in the wind, the mattress was blown across the street, its fiery progress stopped only when it hit the side of an outhouse. The flames jumped from the cotton stuffing to the wood-frame building in seconds.

As they neared Madison Street, the throngs ahead of them thinned, and Nate found he could walk at an almost normal pace. It wouldn't be long before they were turning onto Randolph Street. For the first time, he wondered what he would do if Aunt Ruth wasn't awake waiting for him. He could hardly ask Julie to climb the maple tree. He took a deep breath. It was a relief just to be able to walk, not to be shoved into strangers, constantly bumping into people.

"It's better here," Julie said, looking up at him.

Nate nodded.

A sharp, sudden shout and the sound of a cracking whip made him raise his eyes. A wagoner was standing up, shaking his fist at a group of drunken men who refused to make way.

"Clear off! I have people here who need help bad."

The drunken men stopped to listen, and most of them moved aside. But one man held his ground, swaying on his feet. His companions drew closer, pulling at him, trying to get him to move out of the way. As the driver swore, Nate watched. The man didn't seem to know or care. Nate watched a moment longer, then turned and shot Julie a glance.

She frowned. "What's wrong with them, Nate?"

"Whiskey. And fear, probably."

"Make way! Make way!" The driver was still shouting. The drunken man's friends finally made him move. Nate and Julie stood off to one side, then fell in behind the wagon after it had passed. Nate blinked, his eyes sore from the smoke.

He could see the wounded as the wagon moved away from them. There was an old woman with a bloodied bandage around her head. Next to her sat a boy, his arm in a makeshift sling, a purple bruise disfiguring his shoulder, exposed where his shirt was torn. He sat slumped over, his whole body moving with every jolt of the wagon. As Nate watched, the boy turned, his eyes blank, unfocused. Nate caught his breath. It was Ryan.

Chapter Nine

Just as the wagon of injured people passed, Nate stopped so suddenly that Julie bumped into him. The expression on his face frightened her. "What? What's wrong?"

Nate didn't answer. He began to run. Julie struggled to keep up, fighting her full skirts. She shot a fearful glance back toward the fire, but it was still blocks behind them. "Why are you running?" she demanded, but Nate ignored her.

She stumbled, falling a few strides behind. He didn't slow down at all; he didn't even seem to notice. It looked like he was trying to catch up with the wagon. "Ryan?" she heard him yelling. "Ryan!"

Nate followed the stream of carts and wagons

turning right onto the Madison Street Bridge. Julie sprinted to catch up. "Nate! What are you doing?"

He pointed at the wagon. The driver was standing again to lash the horses back into a gallop. "Wait for me on the other side!"

Without another word, Nate ran on, staying close behind the wagon as it passed between the low barriers that separated the lanes of vehicles. Julie tried to keep up, but couldn't. She slowed, then stopped. She stared as the crowds on the bridge swallowed first the wagon, then Nate.

Standing alone, Julie felt a new fear slide upward along her spine. She let people stream around her, bumping her shoulders as they passed, sometimes cursing her for blocking their way. Then she began to walk again, slowly, filing onto the outer walkway of the bridge, suddenly aware of the worn planks beneath her feet. They were covered with drifting black ash. The river below her was wide and dark— much wider than it had seemed earlier when she and her father had crossed this bridge. Maybe Nate would be back in a few minutes. She said a silent prayer that he wouldn't just leave her here.

"Get out of the way!"

The shout was close and angry, and Julie spun around. There was a tall man carrying a squealing piglet. He was glaring at her. She stepped out of his way, and he went by slowly, catching her eye and grinning. Julie was so unnerved by his sudden smile that it took her a moment to even notice the woman who walked close behind him, her head down, her hair in strings across her face.

As the couple went on, Julie stopped and bit at her lip, trying to calm herself. She would just cross the bridge as Nate had told her to do. She would wait for him for a while, and if he didn't come. . . .

Julie pulled in a deep breath. The end of the Madison Street Bridge opened into Conley's Patch. It was the last place she wanted to be on this awful night. She looked back across the bridge at the traffic on Canal Street. Everyone was running from the fire.

As she started walking again, Julie heard shouts and screams. A ship was ablaze on the west bank. Its rigging burned like straw in the wind, falling, kindling a fire on the deck. Julie could hear the captain shouting orders to his men, but the wind lashed at the flames, and they were spreading fast.

Julie felt a sudden hand on her shoulder and

wrenched away. She glanced sidelong at the crowd. Whoever had touched her was either gone or had no further interest in her. The faces around her were blank, flushed with heat. Julie realized that people were quieter now, most of them walking in silence.

On the east end of the bridge, Julie worked her way to the edge of the crowd until she could stop. She stood on her tiptoes, straining to see farther down Madison Street. The foot traffic was thick, slowing as it had on the other side. People had to maneuver around belongings stacked in the streets.

Julie stood, scanning faces as people came onto the bridge. Why would they be heading toward the fire? Maybe they had relatives on the west side, living in sections where the fire hadn't spread yet. Her uncle Jack lived out on the west edge of the city. Would the fire spread that far? She shuddered.

Cinders and ash were dropping from the sky, then scudding along the ground, tumbled by the wind. The night was lit by the fire, pink and orange, like a false dawn. Julie looked downriver, and her stomach clenched. There were flames on this side of the river now—in the South Division. She heard a man shout, and turned to see him pointing at the new fire.

"That's the Parmelee Building. They don't even have it finished yet. God, what a shame." His companion nodded, and they stood a moment, staring. Then they went on, joining the uneasy parade of people crossing the bridge.

Julie pressed back against the guardrail as another wagon full of wounded people rolled past. Just behind it came a fancy rig, driven by a uniformed coachman. Julie tried to see in the carriage windows—perhaps it was someone she knew, someone who could help her get home. But she didn't recognize the carriage, and the unfamiliar faces inside the windows were all turned back toward the fire, eyes wide. Julie could see a girl gesturing, laughing as the driver sped up to cross the dark chasm of Conley's Patch as quickly as possible.

As the carriage wheeled past her, Julie involuntarily took three or four steps, following it. She felt, somewhere beneath her fatigue and her fear, a strange sense of being out of place. She did not belong on this dirty roadway by herself, her dress filthy and her feet aching. She stared down at the river, the sweet, heavy smell of the water rising to tickle her nose. Her throat ached fiercely, and she wished for a cool glass of water.

"Better be careful, miss," a rough voice said, so close that Julie whirled around, frightened. The man who had grinned at her was standing there, his eyes narrowed as he looked down at her shoes, then up to meet her eyes again. "Shame about that fancy dress."

Julie could feel her heart thudding. "You startled me."

"And I suppose that's a crime where you come from, miss?" The narrow eyes became slits.

Julie wondered where the woman had gone. "It is a crime to bother people in the streets," she said. She meant to sound haughty, the way her mother always did when someone inconvenienced her. But instead, she sounded whiny and scared.

"My woman would give anything for a frock trimmed fancy like the one you have on," the man said, and for an instant his expression was wistful. Then it hardened again. "You'd best come along with me."

Julie shook her head, trying to back up, but his hand shot out, dirty fingers closing around her arm. His grip was painfully tight, and he steered her along, forcing her to walk fast. She tried to pull free, but he held on, talking fast.

"Now don't you be frightened. I won't hurt you. I just want whatever reward your parents are going to pay to get you home safe."

Julie screamed, and three or four people paused midstep, then went on. She struggled, wrenching back and forth, but the man only shifted his grip a little and kept her walking. No one who passed seemed to notice. Their eyes were on the fires.

Just off the bridge, the man turned Julie to the right and pushed her along an alleyway. Julie could see the sad-faced woman standing at the far end. She was holding the piglet now. It wriggled in her arms.

"Hurry up," the woman called. "Someone is going to see."

"No one so much as spoke up when she screamed back there," the man said flatly. "They all have their own worries tonight."

Julie walked four or five paces without struggling, letting her shoulders sag. His grip loosened a little. Abruptly, she whirled and tried to run. The man caught her, spinning her around as though they were dancing.

The woman laughed. "Sweetheart, there is just no use in trying to get away. You are our blessing.

There has to be some good comes from all this." The woman waved one hand in a vague gesture that encompassed the dirty alley, Conley's Patch, the fire.

Julie tried to run again, but the man stopped her. She felt a scream rising in her throat, but it sank again. The man was right. People weren't going to help her; they wouldn't even notice that she needed help.

"Just come along with us," the woman said. She turned to lead the way, and Julie saw a low door set into the end of the alley she hadn't noticed before. The man pushed her through it, and Julie stood uncertainly in the darkness. She could hear them both breathing, then a candle flared to life and she could see the room they had brought her into.

At the sudden light, two rats bolted, disappearing into a hole in the wall. There were sleeping pallets on the floor, three soiled mattresses with tattered blankets on top of each one. Julie's eyes flooded. "I want to go home."

"And that is exactly what you are going to do," the woman said. "Just not quite yet."

Suddenly, Julie heard the courthouse bell begin to toll. Usually, it called the volunteer firemen to their posts, ringing for less than a minute, then fading to silence. This time, it kept tolling, the huge bell hammering out the fire warning like a frantic voice in the night.

Nate stood, braced against the wind, trying to catch his breath. The smoke wasn't as thick here, but it still burned his throat and made him cough. He had run as far and as fast as he could, dodging wagons and people, jumping up onto the boardwalk, then leaping down again—and none of it had done any good.

The driver had kept the horses at a canter all the way across Conley's Patch, then down into the decent part of the South Division. Nate had chased the wagon onto La Salle Street, then had fallen farther and farther behind as the driver had whipped the horses into a full gallop on the nearly empty street. Finally he had lost sight of the wagon altogether.

He turned back, feeling sad and alone. He shivered, hunching his shoulders and pulling his collar tight. Here, away from the fire, the wind was cool, almost chilly. It was dusky, too, the ruddy light of the fire much dimmer.

Nate shook his head angrily. Ryan might get help, but most likely there wouldn't be enough beds or doctors for all the people who needed them tonight. Nate kicked at a pebble. If he could have caught up, he could have made sure that Ryan got water and a blanket—that at least he would be warm.

Nate looked once more in the direction the wagon had gone, then turned back. Still breathing hard, he hurried down La Salle Street. The clanging of the courthouse bell startled him. It continued to ring like a metallic pulse as Nate turned onto Madison.

At the bridge, Nate slowed, expecting to see Julie's bright yellow plaid dress among the drabber colors, but she wasn't there. He started back across the river, watching everyone who came toward him from the Canal Street side. Maybe she had stopped right where he had left her and would see him coming. A few minutes later, he had to admit to himself that she wasn't on the bridge at all.

Nate pulled in a long breath. He had made a terrible mistake in leaving Julie, and he knew it. She had no idea how to take care of herself, and he had put her in grave danger. He pictured her walking with her chin high, her eyes full of anger at him. But then

KATHLEEN DUEY and KAREN A. BALE

what had happened? Had she been foolish enough to walk right off the bridge into Conley's Patch? She would have to be the most sheltered girl in the city not to know what a rough, dangerous place it could be, especially at night. He shook his head. He never should have left her alone.

Turning, he noticed the flames on the east side of the river. There were six or seven men lined up at the guardrail. Two of them wore police uniforms. Another had on the belted rubber coat of a fireman.

Nate walked closer, excusing himself, then waiting until the fireman turned to face him. "Where would be a safe place to go, sir?" Nate asked.

The man looked at him gravely. "The parks, if you can't get any farther. Some are fleeing the city altogether. Do you have a wagon?"

Nate shook his head, stunned. "Is it all going to burn, then?"

The fireman shrugged, and Nate noticed his swollen eyelids. His skin looked boiled. "We were just trying to decide that for ourselves. Most of us seem to think so."

Nate glanced involuntarily to the west, back toward Randolph Street and the boardinghouse.

"You don't think they are going to be able to stop the flames, sir?" he asked, unable to take in the idea of the whole city burning.

"Get whoever and whatever you love to the lakeside, or one of the parks, son. There's not a minute to lose."

The men began talking again. Nate stood numbly for a few seconds, then started running. He had to find Julie, then he had to get home. Somehow, he had to manage both.

Chapter Ten

Julie shook her head, crossing her arms. "No. I won't do it." She was scared, but she tried to keep her voice from shaking.

"Yes, you will," the woman hissed at her. "You'll say we saved you and that you are very grateful to us both."

Julie watched as the piglet nosed through a pile of corn husks in the corner of the room. It had taken Julie a long time to understand why these people would have brought an animal inside, but once she thought about it, it made perfect sense. They had no pen for the piglet because it wasn't theirs. They had stolen it.

"You'll do what we tell you to do," the man said.

He had a softer face than the woman's and he scared Julie less. But he listened to the woman and seemed to go along with whatever she said.

Julie pulled in a deep breath. "My father doesn't keep money in our home." She tried to make herself sound calm. She didn't think they would hurt her, but they might. She wrinkled her nose. More than anything, she wanted to get out of this stinking room. She wanted to go home. Her parents would be frantic.

"If he has no money close to hand, he can just go get some," the woman said angrily. She leered into Julie's face. "He owes us something. You could have fallen into the river if Ned hadn't brought you here. Or you could have gotten into far worse trouble trying to get home alone."

Julie moved away, glancing back and forth between them. The woman looked as bitter and mean as anyone she had ever seen. The man's face was blank. Julie wasn't sure what to do. But if they did take her home, her father would know how to handle them.

"I want to go now," Julie said abruptly. "Right now, or I won't say you saved my life."

"Ned?" The woman kept her eyes on Julie.

"Where do you live?" he asked.

Julie thought about lying, then decided to tell the truth. What was the point in deceiving them? They weren't going to let her go without talking to her father first, anyway. She looked into the woman's eyes. "On Michigan Avenue."

"By the Tremont?" the woman asked sharply.

"No, by the lake," Julie told her.

"A town house? Your father is richer than I thought."

The woman glanced at Ned. He was looking at the pig. "What'll we do with the—"

"We'll leave the animal here," the woman snapped at him. "We can figure out what to do with it later." The woman jammed a tawdry hat onto her head and started toward the door. As she passed Julie, she caught her hand and pulled her along. Julie tried to resist, but it was impossible. The woman's grip was incredibly strong. Ned took Julie's other hand.

Sandwiched between them, Julie stepped outside. The smoky wind swirled around them as they came up out of the alleyway and turned east on Madison Street. Julie wrinkled her nose. They both smelled of tobacco and sweat.

Julie walked slowly, squinting her eyes against the gritty wind, letting the woman pull her along. Men and women filled the street, shouting and drinking. Julie could see the flames of the Parmelee Building and two or three smaller fires, spreading northeast, driven by the constant wind.

As they started up the rise toward Market Street, Julie looked up and saw a slender crescent in the sky. It was the color of embers—it was as though the moon were on fire too.

Nate hesitated at the end of the bridge. A timid girl like Julie wouldn't have gone into Conley's Patch on her own. He stepped aside for a woman who carried an unwieldy length of stovepipe in her arms. She had barely made it past him when a dray, the team keeping up a weary trot, came toward him.

The driver had two people next to him on the bench, a well-dressed couple braced against the wind, looking anxiously from one side to the other. The dray was stacked with rolled carpets, an overturned table with heavy carved legs, a bed frame, and rows of wooden crates. The couple probably had paid the drayman dearly to haul their belongings. Nate hoped the driver would be honest enough to take them as far as he had promised.

A rat dashed across the roadway in front of Nate, a snapping terrier close behind it. Starting forward, Nate saw a trio of people emerge from the alley just ahead of him. He recognized Julie instantly. The other two were strangers. He watched them for a few seconds, then, hiding behind a slow-moving wagon, he worked his way closer. He could see Julie struggling against the woman's grasp.

As the wagon turned up Market Street, Nate came out from behind it and shouted Julie's name. Her face lit with relief as she spun around to face him and he saw the quickness with which the woman pulled her back. The man took a step forward, positioning himself between Nate and Julie.

"What do you want?" The man was big, his clothing stretched over the size of his frame.

Nate hesitated, trying to figure out what he should say.

"Who are you?" the woman demanded. "You're no gentleman's son to be calling her by her Christian name like that."

Nate ducked his head, cursing his own foolishness.

"I work for Miss Julie's family," he said humbly, looking up after an instant. He saw a look of confusion cross Julie's face, then her eyes narrowed. She nodded, a tiny, nearly imperceptible motion. She understood what he was trying to do.

"I work in the family stables, ma'am," Nate told the woman.

She cocked her head to one side. "And why aren't you there now, helping?"

Nate shrugged. "I was taking my Sunday afternoon—I was going to visit my aunt. But with the fire, I ended up having to help her pack up and get out." He let his eyes meet Julie's for an instant, then looked away. Her face was pale. He wanted to help her, he just wasn't sure how.

"We were just walking Miss Julie back home," the woman said, looking at Julie intently. Julie gave a little nod, and the woman smiled. "So we will perhaps see you there."

Nate murmured some polite response and gave Julie a respectful little half bow. Her eyes were full of pleading. He wanted to tell her that he wasn't really going to leave her with these two, but he didn't dare. The woman pulled at Julie's arm and turned her

KATHLEEN DUEY and KAREN A. BALE

around. The big man fell into step and they walked away, Julie a prisoner between them.

Julie glanced back once, and Nate almost waved to reassure her. But then the woman turned around, and he instantly lowered his eyes, pretending not to notice. After a moment he looked southward. The fires were spreading, and they were coming this way. There was no time for an elaborate plan.

Impulsively, Nate turned off Madison onto Fifth Avenue. If he could get around in front of them. . . . Sprinting, pounding along the boardwalk, he made it to the corner of Fifth and the less-traveled half block of Calhoun Street. Ignoring the burn of the smoky air in his lungs, Nate rounded the corner and ran down the narrow boardwalk of Calhoun Street.

Only a few people were walking here, and he passed no wagons at all until he skidded around the next corner, turning right onto La Salle. Praying that his detour would bring him back to Madison Street ahead of Julie, Nate slowed down as he came close to the final corner, then stopped. Breathing hard, he stood in the shadow of an elm tree, watching the flow of people and wagons. After a few seconds, he saw Julie, the man and woman still on either side of her.

As they approached, the woman jerked Julie to one side, yelling at her so loudly that Nate could hear her shrill voice, even though he was almost a block ahead. Julie kept glancing backward. The man put his arm around her shoulders and forced her to face front. She walked between the couple, her head down, her weariness showing in every step. Nate forced himself to wait until they were close. Then he drew in a deep breath and sprinted into the street.

"Julie?" Nate ran up to them. "Julie! I just saw your father. He's up on the corner of Calhoun with a couple of policemen. They were looking for you. Let's go."

Nate saw the woman cast a worried glance at the big man. Before he could react, Nate had hooked his arm through Julie's and was pulling her forward. The woman balked, hanging on tightly to Julie's arm.

Julie was staring into Nate's face. "My father? Oh, I am so grateful to you, Nate." She shook herself free and glared at the woman. When Nate offered her his hand, she took it. He started walking, and she matched his steps. In the distance, a strange rumbling sound swelled, then died.

"We agreed about your father," the woman said loudly, hurrying to keep up.

Nate increased his pace, glancing back at the big man. Julie had bunched her skirts in one hand and was walking fast. A wagon was coming toward them, clattering north on Fifth, the driver a big, fierce-looking Negro man.

Nate glanced back again. The couple was now a half step behind. Their faces were set, grim. "You promised you would talk to your father for us," the man accused. The woman turned and said something to him, her voice low and scolding. The big man nodded and looked up suddenly.

At that instant, Nate squeezed Julie's hand. "Run," he whispered. Julie nodded and pulled him forward, running so fast that it took him three or four strides to match her pace.

"Hey! You come back!" The big man was coming after them, only a few strides behind.

Desperate, Nate glanced around, searching for a way out. The Negro driver met his eyes, and Nate yelled out to him. "Help, please. They're after us!"

The driver hesitated, then reined in. "Jump on the back, children. Be quick."

Nate swerved, using one stiff arm to keep from slamming into the wagon as it slowed. He helped

Julie onto the back, then vaulted up among the stacked boxes, shouting to the driver. Instantly, the team lunged forward again.

Nate lurched, steadying himself with both hands against the wagon gate. Julie let out a little scream, but managed to hang on. She fought with her skirts, rolling dangerously close to the low side rail. Nate grabbed her arm to steady her until she could sit up.

A few seconds later, they were riding along side by side, staring back down Fifth Avenue. The wind slammed against the wagon, cinders and grit like ugly sleet spattering the boxes. The big man had stopped and stood with his hands on his hips. The woman was still running, cursing them with every step.

Nate could still hear the courthouse bell. Had it been ringing all this time? Facing south, he saw pockets of orange-gold flame all over the South Division. Another rumbling sound vibrated through the street planks. Nate could not imagine what would make a noise like that. The wind whistled through the buildings. The firemen had been right. Nothing was going to stop this fire.

Chapter Eleven

The Negro man drove hard; the gale seemed to push the wagon along. As they left Ned and his awful wife behind, Julie sat back and closed her eyes. They stung from the soot and grit in the wind. Her left knee was throbbing. She couldn't remember when she had hurt it.

When she opened her eyes again, Nate was looking over the wagon gate at the fire south of them, just a few blocks away. Julie stared at the flames as they roiled, rising and falling like a crimson curtain. Maybe the fire was gong to burn this side of town, too, all the way to the lake. At least she was getting close to home.

She leaned toward Nate. "Thank you!" She had to

shout over the roaring of the wind. She straightened her skirts, then rubbed at her bruised knee, wincing. "You didn't really find my father, did you?"

Nate shook his head. He looked so apologetic that Julie smiled to let him know she was grateful for his lie. The wagon rumbled over the planks. The streets were less crowded here, but Julie could see people at their windows and atop the roofs, watching and waiting.

The driver pulled the horses back and stopped in front of a brick building. Three or four men started toward the wagon. "This as far as I go, children," he yelled into the wind. "If I was you, I'd get on out of here."

Nate jumped off the wagon, and Julie let him help her down. She called a thanks to the driver, and Nate echoed her words. They got a curt wave in response. The men were already unloading, stacking boxes on the boardwalk.

The sudden, muted, crashing sound was so close that Julie understood for the first time what it had to be. Stone buildings were collapsing in the fire. She took a deep breath and coughed. The smoke stung, and her throat felt raw. "I'm so thirsty," she said aloud.

Nate nodded, hooking his arm through hers. They walked toward the boardwalk as another wagon went past, filled with brown hens. Julie stared into the slatted crates. Most of the chickens were already dead. Nate tugged at her hand, and she turned to face him.

"Where do you live? Where's your house?"

Julie looked at him, then turned in a circle. Nothing seemed familiar to her in the weird reddish glow of the fire. "On Michigan Avenue," she said. "Washington is the cross street," she added, mimicking the directions her mother always gave hansom cab drivers.

Nate was pacing, staring at the fire south of them. "Good. That's northeast of here. We can go up to Washington, then follow it straight east to the lake."

Julie looked at the fire. It was spreading so fast. The roaring was constant now, broken only by the thundering of what had to be another building collapsing. Above all the other noise, the courthouse bell tolled on and on. Julie wiped at her eyes.

"I think the courthouse is on fire," Nate said, pointing. Julie followed his gesture and felt a tremor go through her body. The courthouse was such a big, grand building. It was made of stone. Could it burn?

Julie had been inside it several times with her father. A sudden thought made her cringe. The jails on the floors beneath ground level had prisoners in them all the time, her father had said. Would they be trapped?

"We'd best not stay here!" Nate shouted. "If we don't get across to the lake quick, the fire is going to cut us off!"

Julie turned so that the vicious wind pushed her hair back from her face. She swallowed painfully. "If we can get to my house, my father—"

"Your parents might be gone," he interrupted. "Especially if your father doesn't think you're still alive. And he—"

"It won't matter if they're there," Julie told him. "The lake is just across the street."

"Okay," Nate said, "but I have to get back across the river as soon as I can."

Julie nodded to show him she understood. "I hope your aunt is all right!" she shouted over a sudden rumbling sound that made the street planks vibrate. Nate looked startled, then gestured for her to hurry.

Julie walked as fast as she could. Her knee was aching, and her throat and lungs hurt with every breath. The smoke was getting worse, and every time she glanced over her shoulder, the flames seemed higher and closer, like a rising flood.

They turned right onto Washington Street. Julie could see the courthouse more clearly now. The roof was in flames. The bell still rang out, pealing madly. As they got closer, Julie saw that there were steamers set up all around the big stone building, their hoses throwing water on the fire.

She shoved her hair back from her face. The wind was like a live thing, twisting through the streets, scattering ash and glowing cinders along the planks. The heat was maddening, and her thirst was almost unbearable, and a new misery had worked itself into her consciousness: Her feet hurt. The stiff, polished leather of her shoes had rubbed her ankles raw.

As they passed the courthouse, Nate walked a little slower, staring. Julie dropped back, shortening her own stride to watch. Firemen ran heavily back and forth, shouting and dragging hoses. She saw one man stumble, barely managing to right himself. Up on the boardwalk across the street, an old man with a gray beard ran a zigzagging course, his coat on fire. Julie watched him drop into a horse trough to put out the flames.

She forced herself to keep going. The air here was so hot she put one hand over her nose and mouth. As they passed the courthouse, her skin stung and pinpricks of pain marked where tiny cinders struck her face and hands. A rhythmic thudding made her look back. Men were battering down a door at one end of the courthouse.

She gestured questioningly, and Nate turned to look, then shrugged. A moment later Julie understood. Prisoners were streaming up from the cells beneath the courthouse. Most of them staggered outside, then began to run, fanning out. A few were handcuffed and forced to march eastward with a guard. Julie walked a little closer to Nate until they had passed.

The scorching air made it hard to breathe, but Julie knew their only hope was to hurry. "My God," Nate yelled suddenly. Julie turned to see him pointing. Only two blocks south of them, Madison Street was carpeted with glowing coals. There was a man trying to run across them, screaming. She looked aside, sickened. Nate grabbed her arm, and they staggered on under the pressing weight of the increasing heat.

◇ ◇ ◇

Nate wasn't sure he could go on much farther. But he knew what would happen if he gave up. He stepped around a dead dog in the street and scrambled up onto the boardwalk. Julie climbed up after him, her skin reddened beneath the soot on her face. Her stockings were torn, and he noticed for the first time that they were heavy wool—riddled with burns from the wind-driven cinders. And it was only getting worse.

The screaming wind carried so many sparks that they swirled like insane fireflies, whipping around the corners of the buildings, scattering in fans along the boardwalk. Everything was smoking or on fire.

At the corner of State Street, a hideous crashing thundered up the street behind them, swallowing the sound of the roaring flames, the wind, even the terrified thudding of Nate's own heart. The ground trembled beneath his feet, and Julie screamed. Nate looked back. The courthouse tower had fallen in, smashing its way through the core of the building. For the first time in hours, the bell was silent.

An invisible wall of heat rolled through the air, scorching Nate's face. He heard Julie cry out, and he turned to see her slapping at her billowing skirts. He dropped to his knees and helped, crushing the cloth between his hands, brushing the smoldering hemline until the fire was out.

When he stood, Julie was crying. She fought her skirts in the wind, gathering them, then took his hand and led off. They stepped over a burning plank that skidded along the wind-whipped street.

"I know the way from here!" Julie yelled over the sound of the wind. Nate glanced back the way they had come. The courthouse was invisible now, hidden behind a raging red sheet of fire.

"Look out!" Julie yanked him to one side.

He faced forward and saw that a portion of the boardwalk had collapsed. He had almost run headlong into broken planks that jutted up from underneath.

The First National Bank was afire as they passed. Nate saw a steamer set up on the corner. The firemen's coats gave off a strong burned-rubber odor that made Nate cover his mouth and nose with his free hand. He thought about the lake and imagined himself running into the cool water, sinking beneath the surface until his skin stopped stinging.

The people they passed were all silent now, grim. Some were carrying their worldly goods in their arms; many more had wagons or carriages. Nate and Julie passed three or four buildings that weren't yet in flames. The heat diminished a little. Nate rubbed his eyes hard, clearing his vision. He looked at Julie. Her face was still flushed deep red, but she was walking a little faster, a look of determination on her face.

"Oh, no," Julie cried out as they came to the corner. Nate followed her anguished gesture. Down State Street, Booksellers Row was in flames. A few people dodged in and out of the shop doors, carrying books, and he wondered if Julie was remembering Mr. Black.

Nate squeezed her hand. "Julie! Where's your house?"

"Up there," Julie said, pointing. She led the way, jumping off the boardwalk onto Michigan Avenue, plunging into the crowds that were moving toward Lake Park.

Across the street, Nate could see the fire reflected in Lake Michigan. The surface was choppy, and the flames glittered in a wind-shattered mirror. Nate stared at the expanse of dark water beyond the reflections and ached with thirst and heat. It was so crowded that it was hard to find a path through the people and wagons that choked Michigan Avenue. But at least the fire wasn't here yet, and the heat was less intense.

Nate had to hurry to keep up with Julie. He saw two little girls, the elder probably no older than five, huddled together along the side of the street. He tried to see their parents as he passed and could not. Walking sideways, he ran into someone.

"Watch out!"

Nate felt a heavy hand on his shoulder and looked up to see a tall, scowling man. Half his scalp was bare, the skin patched with red and black. He shoved his way past.

Julie had slipped between a hansom cab and a wagon full of crying children. Nate followed her, seeing for the first time that her hair had been badly singed in back. It was ragged, three inches shorter on one side.

"Just up here," Julie said over her shoulder.

Nate tried to see past her, but the crowd was too thick. After a minute or so, she turned again and pointed. Nate saw a row of town houses, their shining white exteriors grayed by the smoke. Nate followed her, weaving through the boxes and trunks stacked close to the street.

Julie went up a flight of stairs. Nate followed her to a set of wide, carved, double doors. Julie pulled a key from beneath a pot of geraniums, and Nate waited as she unlocked the doors and swung them open.

He stood at the threshold as Julie ran across the stone-floored entryway, then disappeared up a carpeted stairway. He could hear her calling for her parents, could hear the rising panic in her voice. When she came back down, her face was streaked with tears. She carried a sheet of white paper in one hand.

"My parents are gone," she told him, lifting the paper so that he could see the even, bold script as she began to read aloud in a hoarse, rasping voice.

"'Dearest Julie, my greatest fear is that you are lost to us. My greatest hope is that you are not. If you make it to the house and the fire is not too close, stay here. I will come for you as soon as your mother is safe at your uncle Jack's. I have left money if you need it to hire a carriage or other aid. There is water and food in the kitchen. I pray to God that you are safe.'"

Julie held out a bank note. Nate could see that her hand was shaking.

"Julie," Nate began. His throat ached, and he swallowed painfully. "Is there water?"

She seemed startled, then apologized, turning down a hallway that led past the stairs. He followed a few steps, then stopped. The carpets were beautiful, with intricate patterns. His shoes were filthy.

Julie came back toward him carrying two glasses full of water and handed him one. He drank greedily as she spoke. "The spigot isn't working. Father left a pail by the washbasin. He must have thought that—"

"Is there more?" Nate interrupted her. His throat was so raw that the cool water had been like heaven as it slid down. Julie motioned for him to follow her, and he stepped carefully across the carpets.

It felt strange to be out of the wind, to stand still. Nate filled and refilled his glass, drinking fast. It was unnaturally hot, but standing in the clean, spacious kitchen, it was almost possible to forget the fire for an instant.

The sound of the crowd outside was muted through the heat-cracked windows. To the west, Nate could see a stable; it looked askew through the shattered glass.

"I should wait here for my father," Julie said. There was a note of uncertainty in her voice.

Nate could see the fear in Julie's eyes. "If it was safe here, they wouldn't have left. Julie, the fire is *close*." He waited until she met his eyes. "We'll get back across the river and find my aunt. With any luck, the fire won't spread up that way."

Julie wiped at her face, leaving black streaks on her cheeks. "What if we can't get back across? Nate, for all we know, your aunt has already left too. Maybe your boardinghouse is gone by now." Her voice was small, rising and falling with each breath. "And the lake is right here."

Nate shrugged. "You can stay, but I don't have a choice, Julie. I have to get home. If you come with me, I'll help you get to your uncle's place once I know Aunt Ruth is all right."

A rolling crash made them both spin around, facing the west window. A rising cloud of smoke and dust obscured some of the flames for a moment.

"The buildings are all crumbling under the heat." Julie's voice seemed a little steadier.

"We should leave now," Nate said, feeling incredibly tired. He looked into Julie's frightened eyes. "You could go straight to the lake." He hesitated, trying to think clearly. "It might be smarter, Julie." A second rolling shudder passed through the ground. Another big building had fallen.

Julie shook her head. "I'll go with you. I know where Father keeps his hunting gear. He has a canteen."

Nate nodded and pointed at the stables. "Is that your father's?"

"Yes," Julie said. "But he might not have left the horses behind if he thought it was going to burn."

Nate nodded. "If there is a horse, can you ride?"

"Yes. Sidesaddle, or astride. My uncle Jack taught me."

"Good. What's the quickest way down to the stables?"

Julie showed him a side door. He opened it. Smoke and noise poured into the house. Julie caught his sleeve as he went past her. "I'll fill the canteen, then come down there as quick as I can."

Nate saw an odd look in her eyes and realized

that she was still terrified. Awkwardly, he reached out to squeeze her hand. "We'll make it out, Julie. Just hurry."

Nate ran along a stone walk, then followed a little path that led around a garden and down to the stables. He could hear a horse inside, whinnying anxiously. There were poplar trees around the paddock, and the ground was strewn with broken limbs. He lifted the lock bar and let the big double doors fly open, the wind holding them flat against the wall.

All the stalls were standing open. They were all empty except for one. In the last stall, a gelding stood trembling, its eyes circled in white, its nostrils flared. Nate glanced around the barn. Buckets had been knocked over, a saddle had been thrown aside and lay on the hay. It was obvious that the horses had been moved in a hurry. The remaining gelding had likely refused to move, terrified by the smell of smoke, too frightened to leave the safety of its barn.

Nate approached the gelding slowly, talking quietly. The horse turned to face him, its ears pitched forward. Nate took one step, then paused, then a second step, talking gently the whole time. Slowly, Nate worked his way closer to the gelding.

Nate knew it would be dangerous to ride a terrified horse through the smoky streets with the flames roaring closer. But the horse would save them precious time, too. "Steady, boy, steady," Nate murmured, trying to keep his voice calm. He took one more step and caught the gelding's halter in his hand. To his surprise, the horse stepped toward him, nudging his arm. "You're ready to get out of here now, aren't you, boy?" Nate asked softly, leading the gelding out of the stall.

Nate found a feed sack that would serve as a saddle blanket, and a bridle that he managed to let out to fit the gelding. At the barn door, the gelding reared, but Nate calmed him down and talked him into edging outside into the hot wind.

Blinking in the weird reddish light, the gelding stood, trembling, as Nate looked toward the house. Julie was coming down the path toward him. Behind her, less than a quarter mile away, a towering wall of flame lit the night sky.

Chapter Twelve

The scalding wind hit Julie as she came out the door carrying her father's old army canteen. She glanced at the approaching wall of fire, then followed the path around the garden. Nate was standing just outside the stable door. He had saddled her father's new gelding and stood holding the reins tightly in one hand. The instant he saw her, he gestured toward the flames, then motioned her to hurry. Julie began to run, the canteen banging against her side.

When she reached him, Nate was patting the horse's neck, trying to calm it down.

"It might be best if I ride in front. I'm stronger."

Julie nodded. Nate boosted her up and waited until she had managed to arrange her skirts. Then he pulled the nervous gelding around in a tight circle, finally getting his foot into the stirrup. She leaned back to let him swing his leg over, then straightened again. Without warning, the gelding surged forward. Julie grabbed at Nate's waist, hoping he could control the frightened animal.

For a few seconds, all Julie could do was hang on. Then, Nate hauled the gelding back into a slow canter. Julie leaned forward and shouted into Nate's ear, "That path leads up to Michigan Avenue." She pointed to the dirt track that led through the poplar trees.

Nate swung the gelding around and gave it enough rein to canter up the slope. Julie loosened her arms around Nate's waist and tried to let the rhythm of the horse's gait take over, the way her uncle had taught her. It was hard; she was so tired and so scared that every muscle in her body felt tightly strung.

Nate rode north on Michigan Avenue, and Julie could tell he was fighting to slow the gelding down. It danced sideways on the plank-covered roadway, tossing its mane, very nearly knocking down a woman with a baby in her arms. The woman's husband shouted a warning, then an insult as Nate guided the gelding past them.

Julie leaned to look past Nate and almost cried out. She could feel her heart thudding in her chest. The flames were ahead of them as well as behind. Lake Park was jammed with people, some of them standing knee-deep in Lake Michigan. As Nate headed north, as fast as the crawling traffic would allow, Julie saw a number of wagons that had been driven straight into the shallows. The horses stood belly deep in the water; the drivers' legs were submerged. The vicious heat made Julie stare, entranced, at the people who had gone into the water. At least they were safe from the fire.

The gelding balked suddenly, sidling backward, drawing curses and shouts from people behind them. Nate worked to straighten the horse out, and Julie leaned to see what was wrong.

Just in front of the gelding, a man had collapsed. Two women were struggling to lift him. Nate eased the nervous gelding to one side, skirting them. People stepped over the man, unable to make the crowd on either side give them room enough to go around. Julie looked back, but the crowd had closed and she couldn't see anything.

Facing forward again, Julie stretched up and

found she could just peek over Nate's shoulder. There was a dark corridor to the east, even though the flames straight ahead of them were spreading, the wind continuing its lashing gusts. The street was less crowded here, and Julie was glad when Nate let the gelding canter again. Half a block farther on, he had to rein in.

The shoreline of the lake was lined with people and their belongings, piled close to the water's edge. Julie saw a man digging madly in the sand. Astonished, she saw him positioning two small children in the hole. Was he going to bury them to protect them from the heat? She twisted in the saddle to try to see what he was doing. At her last glimpse he was pitching sand back into the hole.

"Hang on!" Nate yelled over his shoulder.

Julie tightened her grip on his waist just as the horse bolted forward. At first, she thought something had scared it, but then she realized that Nate was digging his heels into the horse's sides. As the gelding pounded along the plank-covered street, Julie managed to get a glimpse over Nate's shoulder. The street ahead of them was empty—but it was bordered on both sides by fire.

As they got closer to the leaping flames, the gelding stiffened its strides, raising its head and slowing down. Nate drummed at the horse's ribs and flanks with his heels, shouting encouragement.

Julie stared at the tunnel of fire they were about to enter. The flames were so close here, arcing almost all the way over the street. The burning buildings were sagging beneath the weight of their brick and stone facades. The gelding slowed a little more, and Julie heard Nate's voice rise to a panic pitch. She knew why. If the gelding balked here, they would have little chance of survival. She loosened one hand from around Nate's waist and slipped her father's canteen strap from her shoulder.

Then, careful of her balance, Julie let go with her other hand. Holding the canteen itself close to her body, she gripped the long strap in her right hand. Suddenly she shrieked like a dime novel Indian on the warpath and whipped at the horse's flanks, lashing it with the long leather strap. Startled, the gelding leaped forward, lunging to get away from the sudden attack of stinging pain.

The high flames on either side of them slid past as the horse raced forward. The air seared at Julie's lungs, and she could hear the gelding dragging in heat-barbed breaths. She could feel the horse trembling even as it galloped, but it did not balk again, and in seconds, they burst out of the tunnel of fire.

Nate pulled the gelding in a wide turn, risking a quick backward glance to grin at Julie. She smiled back at him, tremors of fear still vibrating down her arms and legs. The gelding galloped on as she resettled the canteen. She held tightly to Nate's waist, feeling an odd lightness in her heart, a quickening of hope as they turned onto Randolph Street and headed west into the tearing wind.

Showers of sparks and embers burst over the rooflines of the buildings that lined Randolph. Julie could see sheets of flame snapping like giant, tattered flags, shredded by the force of the wind.

Nate kept the gelding at a gallop, swerving to avoid people in the street. In front of the Field and Leiter's store, Julie saw a wagon. It was loaded with what looked like brocade dresses and bales of silk. The driver was lashing the horses, shouting at the top of his voice. The wind drowned out his words, but the sharp pops of the whip reached Julie's ears. She stared as they went past.

Men were standing in front of Field and Leiter's, passing buckets along a line. The marble front of the building looked wet. Nate swerved abruptly, and Julie clutched at his waist, realizing only after a moment that another wagoner, coming out of a side street, had whipped his team directly into their path.

"Hang on!" Nate screamed over his shoulder. The gelding changed leads, trying to veer sharply enough. Then it stumbled, pitching forward, but managed to right itself. Julie clung to Nate's back as they were flung forward, trying not to lose her balance, terrified that she would start to slide sideways. An instant later, the gelding was running solidly again. Julie pressed her face against Nate's shoulder, her eyes closed for a few seconds. When she opened them, the wagon was a half block behind them.

Nate pulled the gelding in as they crossed State Street. Julie could see the posters displayed around the grand entrance of the Crosby Opera House. The paper had burst into flames from the heat in the air.

For an instant Julie pictured the tickets on her mother's bureau. Julie knew her parents had been looking forward to the Crosby Opera House's reopening tomorrow night. The Theodore Thomas

Orchestra was to have been featured. The opera house had been newly furnished with fine carpets and bronzes. For weeks, the sound of hammers and saws had rung out from the wide entry doors. Now, the opera house would probably be destroyed.

Julie heard a rending scream. Up ahead, a woman stood in front of Wood's Museum. The hem of her dress was aflame, and she seemed unable to do anything about it beyond her wailing. Julie felt Nate rein in. As the gelding slowed, fighting the bit, Julie's eyes were riveted on the screaming woman. Nate swung his leg over the horse's neck and then pulled Julie to the ground. He handed her the reins and she stood, gripping the leather tightly as the gelding circled nervously.

Nate sprinted away from her, tearing off his shirt. He dragged it through an ash-clotted water trough, then leaped up onto the boardwalk. Falling to his knees, he beat at the woman's flaming skirts. She seemed to understand that he was trying to save her and she turned slowly, still screaming hysterically, her arms straight up in the air.

Suddenly, the gelding reared, startling Julie so badly that she nearly let go of the reins. She jumped aside, hauling the horse back down as she had often seen her father do. For a moment, she concentrated on keeping hold of the reins, talking quietly to calm herself as much as the horse. Her hands were shaking. The gelding stood nervously, its ears twitching back and forth.

When she managed to look back at Nate and the woman again, the flames were out. The woman was shaking her head as Nate gestured down Randolph Street. Abruptly, her blackened skirt swirling around her legs, she turned and ran—eastward toward Michigan Avenue. The gelding danced sideways, and Julie had to fight to control it again.

"Where is she going?" Julie shouted as Nate came toward her, putting on his wet shirt.

"Her family is by the lake," Nate said, breathing hard. "Here, Julie." He laced his fingers into a stirrup.

Julie let him help her mount, then leaned back to give him room to swing his leg over. She barely had time to get her arms around his waist before the gelding leaped into a headlong gallop again. By the time they passed Miller's Jewelry Store, Nate had the gelding in hand. A little farther on, Julie stared at the collapsed ruin that had been the courthouse.

Suddenly, the gelding shied, dropping back into a trot, jarring her so badly that she slewed to one side. Nate half turned, reaching back to steady her. "Hold on! It's going to get worse up here."

He faced front again, and Julie leaned to look ahead of them. The stream of people was thickening on Randolph Street. The gelding was nervous, tossing its head as Nate wove a crooked path between wagons and wheelbarrows, makeshift stretchers, and an endless current of frightened people.

As they crossed Fifth Avenue, Nate was forced to rein in again. On all sides of them, a crush of refugees slowed as they all neared the bottleneck of the Randolph Street Bridge. Julie could hear Nate talking to the gelding, a constant, soothing rush of words. The horse was sweating, lathered. It was high-spirited and swift, Julie knew—too highly bred to be docile when it was boxed in like this.

"Get out of the way!"

At the sound of the enraged shout, Julie stretched up to see over Nate's shoulder. A big man was shaking his fist, cursing at a woman who sat woodenly on the driver's bench of a hansom cab. How she had come to be driving it was a mystery. Julie had certainly never seen a woman driving a hack before.

At first, Julie couldn't tell what the problem was, but it was clear that the traffic behind the wagon was standing still. More men began to shout, and so did a few of the women. Nate guided the gelding closer to the gutter, where traffic was still moving. The people close behind the hansom had no such choice. The crowds on either side were packed too tightly, and no one seemed willing to let them get into line.

Slowly, Julie and Nate came up alongside the hansom. When Julie saw what the problem was, she caught her breath. The horse pulling the hansom had died in its harness. It lay at a strange angle, one foreleg cocked upward, its eyes closed. Julie felt Nate recoil and saw him look aside. She could not, even though it was awful. The poor animal had probably run miles that night and had finally dropped of exhaustion.

Julie looked into the woman's face. She had no expression at all and she sat so still that for a second Julie thought perhaps she had fainted. But her face wasn't pale, and her eyes were wide open. Julie heard another curse and saw the big man clambering around the hansom. Looking back as they passed,

Julie saw him raise a knife, then bend to cut the harness. Four or five other men were standing close, shouting back and forth. Julie faced front again.

For a moment, Julie stared at the back of Nate's shirt. The roar of the wind was loud enough to drown out most of the crowd's noise. She glanced up at the sky. The weird glowing flakes of falling debris streamed and swirled in the wind. The eerie orangish light of the fire still arced against the sky, but it was a little less hellish now.

Julie closed her eyes for a second, suddenly understanding. The fire had not dimmed; the sky was getting brighter. It was a half hour or so before dawn.

Chapter Thirteen

Nate fought to keep the gelding calm—to keep himself calm. It was unnerving to be trapped in the living mass that filled Randolph Street from gutter to gutter. The wind was so strong now that he had to squint to be able to see anything at all. His shirt was molded against his side, held there by the violent gusts. The gelding's mane lashed his hands, stinging his skin.

Nate strained to see the far side of the river. Stray pockets of fire seemed to be everywhere, but there were no walls of flame yet. Maybe the boardinghouse would be all right. Maybe.

Nate remembered the canteen and felt a sudden, piercing thirst. He could feel Julie's hands trembling on his waist as he turned. "May I have a drink?" He spoke loudly so that she could hear him over the wind and the crowd.

Abruptly, the gelding danced sideways, barely missing a tall, grim-faced man on their right. Nate twisted back around, tightening the reins. The gelding steadied, and Nate was grateful. The tall man was carrying a pistol.

Nate glanced over his shoulder again to take the canteen from Julie. He tipped it up for a long drink. The water was incredibly cool—soothing his smoke-raw throat. As he lowered the canteen, he saw a man looking at it greedily. Lowering it quickly, Nate let it rest on the saddle. He held it there until the man looked away. Then he handed it back to Julie.

The crowd was inching forward. Nate kept patting the gelding's neck, trying to ease its natural fear of the people pressing close on all sides. Nate could see the Randolph Street Bridge clearly now. The roadway was marked with flat-topped railings that ran between the buggy lanes. On a normal day, there could be as many as ten carriages or wagons on the bridge at the same time. Today, there would be thirty or more, hemmed in on every side by people walking, pushing wheelbarrows and handcarts, dragging trunks loaded with heavy silverware and other family treasures.

The plank walkways that ran outside the buggy road—outside the big, wagon wheel supports—were jammed with people. Nate heard shouting and saw that the guardrail on the right side was broken. People were moving onto the bridge carefully, pressing against the arched supports that separated them from the wagon roadway. They walked sideways, their eyes on the river below.

The crowd moved forward again. The gelding took a step, then stopped again. Nate patted its neck. The muscles beneath the silky coat were tight as piano strings. The big horse was trembling, its shoulders dark with sweat.

"Can you see if there's fire on the other side of the bridge?" Julie asked.

Nate glanced back at her, shaking his head. "No, not this far up."

Julie didn't answer. He saw a look of deep sorrow in her eyes.

"Your parents are probably fine."

"I hope so. I—"

A scream cut short her answer. They both faced front, Julie leaning to see around him. Nate watched, horrified, as a man pitched off the bridge walkway where the guardrail was broken. A woman tried to catch his arm but could not. She wailed, appealing to those behind her for help. Shrugging, avoiding her eyes, the crowd streamed past her.

"Oh, God, Nate!"

He nodded without turning to look at Julie. There was nothing they could do. The crowd surged forward five or ten feet, and Nate had to concentrate on keeping the gelding in hand. The high-strung animal would bolt, given any chance at all. And if it did, it would end up trampling someone.

As they came to the rise in the roadway that would funnel them onto the bridge, Nate looked downstream, hoping to catch a glimpse of the man who had fallen. There were tugboats near the bridge. Maybe the man had been hauled aboard one of them. Nate hoped so.

"Look!" Julie was pointing upriver.

Nate followed her gesture. The Madison Street Bridge had been swung open, its spans folded like wings around its central support. People on both sides of the river were yelling at the bridge tender, pleading with him to swing the spans back into place so they could cross. Nate shook his head. As long as the bridge tender ignored them, the people were trapped.

The gelding shuddered when its hooves touched the bridge planking, but stepped cautiously up behind the freight wagon in front of them. The people walking made their way to one side or the other, using the boardwalks outside the roadway lanes. Those who went to the right passed the broken railing in single file.

Nate sat in the saddle alertly, ready for any sudden move the horse might make. There was no room for error. If the gelding acted up here, it could easily blunder into a barricade, crushing their legs. Only once they were well onto the bridge, moving with the snail-slow traffic, did Nate risk another glance at the river.

A ship, pulled by tugs, was heading upstream, past the open Madison Street Bridge. Beyond it, Nate could see the Van Buren Street Bridge, a smoking skeleton, its spans destroyed. Smoke hazed the air as the wind buffeted them, only a little cooler as they crossed the water. On the west side, the traffic was choking the narrow bridge approach, and Nate fought an urge to force the gelding through the hordes of refugees.

"Nate!"

Startled, Nate twisted in the saddle at the sound of the familiar voice. He scanned the crowd, his eyes passing over a hundred pale, ash-streaked faces.

"Nate!"

This time Nate recognized Ryan's voice and managed to spot him. He was walking on the pedestrian's boardwalk on the far side of the bridge. He raised one hand, waving.

"That boy—" Julie began, tugging Nate's sleeve.

"That's Ryan," Nate interrupted happily. "He's all right!"

Glancing at Ryan every few seconds, Nate guided the gelding uphill, waiting for a chance to angle across the street. Ryan smiled and waved every time their eyes met. When the traffic thinned out a little, Nate held the gelding in to keep from leaving Ryan behind. They were almost a block past the bridge before Nate managed to work his way to the side of the street, closing the distance between them.

Nate slid off the gelding and helped Julie down. "I saw you," he told Ryan. "I saw you in one of those wagons and I thought you were hurt bad." He stopped as he looked into Ryan's dull, exhausted eyes.

"I was," Ryan said slowly. "For a while, I wasn't sure what my own name was. But I'm pretty sure my arm is just sprained." Ryan wriggled his fingers, then lifted his arm, wincing. "See? I can move everything."

Julie made a little sound, and Nate turned to see her staring at Ryan's ugly bruises. He introduced her to Ryan, then patted the horse's neck.

"Julie and I can walk awhile. You ride the gelding. I'll lead him," he added quickly, seeing the look of uncertainty on Ryan's face.

Nate helped Ryan into the saddle, and they set off again. Julie walked quietly with her head down. She took a drink from the canteen and offered it to Nate. He shook his head and passed it up to Ryan. Ryan drank noisily, spilling water down his filthy shirtfront. Nate pushed the cork back into the canteen and handed it to Julie once more. He glanced upward. The sky was hazy with smoke, but the light of dawn was shining through.

"My father is going to kill me," Ryan said softly.

Nate shook his head. "No, he won't. Aunt Ruth might kill me, though."

Nate heard Julie take in a long breath. For the rest of the way up the rise to Canal Street, she kept glancing westward. Nate followed her gaze. She was probably thinking about her parents. He hoped they were all right.

As they got closer, Nate could see that the block the boardinghouse was on had been untouched by the fire. The trees had not escaped the heat, though. They were scorched, wilting.

"Your aunt Ruth's place looks all right," Ryan said. "And I don't see any burn farther on. My family might just be all right, too."

Nate grinned at him. "It looks that way." He felt his heart lighten in his chest. But where was Aunt Ruth? It was hard to believe that she and all the boarders were inside, no one even watching the progress of the fire.

"Where is everyone?" Julie wondered, speaking his thought. Nate shrugged, leading the gelding up the drive. In the early morning sunlight, the poplars cast their shadows across the road. Nate glanced up at the second-story windows. He saw Mr. Dwight's broad, friendly face. As the heavyset man turned from the window, Nate heard him shout.

"Go tell her you're safe," Ryan said, wincing with pain as he dismounted. "I'm going to head on home."

"No," Nate said. "Wait for me. You shouldn't walk."

Ryan shook his head. "My legs are fine. They're about the only part of me that doesn't hurt. I'll be by to see you when my pa lets me out of the doghouse."

Nate nodded and watched Ryan cross the street. Then he handed Julie the reins and started toward the porch. Before he was halfway up the steps Aunt Ruth flung open the front door.

"Are you all right, Nathan?"

He nodded, but before he could say anything, she gripped his shoulders, peering into his face, her eyes flooded with tears. She hugged him quickly, then held him at arm's length. "When I saw that you weren't in your bed, I was so frightened. Then I got angry. I've been worried sick, Nathan Cooper."

Mr. Oliver pushed open the door and limped out onto the porch. His eyes were still badly swollen. "Your aunt paced the hallway all night long."

"I'm sorry," Nate said, staring down at his ash-grayed shoes. He rubbed one against his trouser leg, then switched feet to try to clean the other one.

"Never mind your shoes, Nathan," Aunt Ruth said. "I want your promise that you'll never go out that window again."

Nate looked up. "I promise," he said.

Aunt Ruth was looking past him. "And who is this?"

Nate watched Julie smooth her ruined skirt. "I'm Julie Flynn. Nate saved my life."

Nate glanced at his aunt. She was beaming. "My Nate is a brave one. Maybe too brave. Where are your folks, child?"

Julie smiled. "At my uncle Jack's place. Miles west of here."

Aunt Ruth nodded. "As soon as you have rested up, we can help you find them. You must be hungry. There are biscuits and gravy left from breakfast and a chocolate cake from last night's supper."

Nate's stomach clenched, and he realized how hungry he was.

Julie's eyes had gone wide. "Chocolate cake?"

Mr. Oliver made a shooing motion with his hands. "Go on in. I'm just going to stand out here a little while and see what's what."

Nate nodded. Mr. Oliver met his eyes. "We could have used your help. There was a storm of cinders those first few hours."

When Nate didn't answer, Mr. Oliver clapped him gently on the shoulder. "Sounds like that girl needed help, too. I'm just glad you're safe, son."

Nate stood still, letting it seep in. Ryan was all right. Julie would be fine once she was back with her parents. He looked up at the porch. He could see Aunt Ruth waiting just inside the front door. Nate grinned. He had made it home.

Turn the page for more
survival stories in

Gavin Reilly stood on the boat deck of the Titanic, his eyes closed tightly. He gripped the handrail and counted to ten. Then he opened his eyes again. He had to get over this. He *had* to get used to looking out over the open water. After a few dizzying seconds, he turned landward, gulping huge breaths of the cool air. He stared at the coastline and the green hills above Queenstown, Ireland. This was ridiculous. He had been swimming since he was a baby He had never been afraid of water in his life.

"Are you all right?"

Gavin looked up to see a girl with light brown hair, and a scattering of freckles across the bridge of her nose. She looked concerned. Her accent, broadly American, sounded brash and rude.

"Are you sick?"

Gavin shook his head. There was no way to explain what was wrong with him. He didn't really understand it himself. "I'm fine," he said, staring back at the shoreline.

The town's docks were all too small for the *Titanic*, so the enormous liner had been anchored two miles offshore. Passengers, goods, and mailbags were being brought out to her. Gavin watched the tenders and bumboats scuttling back and forth. The *Ireland* was not a small boat, but it looked like a toy beside the *Titanic*. The *America* stood off a little distance, waiting its turn to unload.

Gavin watched a bumboat come alongside. Most of them were loaded with Irish goods. The first-class nabobs and their finely dressed wives would have their chance to buy Irish linen and lace, even if they couldn't go ashore.

Gavin glanced sideways. The girl was still standing nearby, but she was looking out to sea now, her hair blowing in the wind. Gavin wanted more than anything to turn and face the open water, but he knew he couldn't. He moved a little ways away from the girl, hoping she wouldn't follow.

Gavin leaned against the metal railing. The familiar green curve of the south Irish coast was less than two miles away over the water. He stared at Queenstown with its narrow streets and closely packed buildings. He sighed.

The hills behind the town were so green, they reminded him of his home outside Belfast. He could imagine his brothers and sisters tending the potato patch in the high pasture. Sean's voice would be ringing out over little Katie's giggles. Gavin could almost see her, freckled and pink-faced. Liam would be arguing with Mary, The little ones would be with Mother at home, lined up on her cot for noontime nap. Gavin felt the now-familiar physical ache that always accompanied thoughts of his family. He might never see them again.

"Are you ill?" the girl asked.

Gavin glanced at her and shook his head, then pointedly turned his back. He forced himself to look out to sea. The cold gray water stretched all the way to the horizon. He wasn't sure why it bothered him so much. Everyone agreed the *Titanic* was unsinkable. That very morning they had run a full dress rehearsal emergency; alarms sounding, they had closed all the watertight doors.

Gavin had been so determined to get a position on the *Titanic* that he had traveled to Southampton, lied about his age, and stood in line with several hundred others to be interviewed. Conor's letters from New York had set him dreaming of a different life. Like all older brothers, Conor wanted him to have opportunities, too. Their mother had lit a candle for Conor the day he had sailed for America. Now she would light two every Sunday. The idea of the candles made Gavin feel a sharp stab of homesickness.

"I didn't mean to intrude," the girl said apologetically. He glanced at her, about to apologize for his own rudeness, but she had already turned away.

He watched her walk past the gigantic funnel that jutted up at an angle from the deck. The other three were real and spouted black smoke when the *Titanic* was underway. This one was fake, nothing more than a huge air vent. Still, like the others, it was anchored with thick steel cables. Gavin saw the girl start down the steep stairs toward the third-class promenade.

"Hey, Gavin! You'd better get back down to the galley." Lionel's voice startled him. The tall, blond-haired boy dropped onto one of the wooden benches along the handrail. "Mr. Hughes will see you slacking, and they'll be booting you off. That would shame your roommates, you know."

Gavin grinned. "I would hate to do that."

"Well, Harry and I would be shamed at any rate. I'm not sure Wallace has it in him."

They both laughed. "I've only been up here a few minutes," Gavin said. "I needed fresh air."

Lionel shrugged. "Are you seasick? At anchor? It's going to be like sailing a whole city across the Atlantic, Gavin. She barely rolls at all."

Gavin shot one more glance at the open water and felt his stomach tighten. "I'd better get started washing the new potatoes. First class is going to have them boiled *parmentier*."

"Work hard and you can end up a first-class steward like me." Lionel stood up straight, clowning, squaring his shoulders in exaggerated pride. "I have to go down to the dining room to deliver a message."

"I'll go down with you," Gavin said, getting to his feet. Together they headed toward the second-class entrance. Gavin reached out to open the door. Side by side they started down the long stairway. Their steps were timed to a rhythmic patter that kept them moving downward at almost a running pace. Lionel had taught Gavin how to run the stairs like this and he shot him a grin of approval. "You're getting good."

Gavin grinned back, feeling better.

As they descended past the windows of the Palm Court, he saw the first-class passengers seated in the elaborately decorated garden room. There were a few men onboard who were so wealthy, their clothing had probably cost more than it took to feed Gavin's family for a whole year. He had seen one woman wearing a necklace of diamonds so big, they shot glitters across the room.

On the B-deck landing, Gavin could smell the heavy scent of tobacco coming from the second-class smoking room. Lionel lifted one hand to cover his nose and mouth. Gavin nodded. First-class was the worst—expensive cigars had a pungent odor that clung to the very walls.

As they went deeper into the ship, Gavin felt his nervousness subside a little. Down here, the *Titanic* was much like a grand hotel. It was easier to forget the deep gray water that would soon separate him from his family and from the farm where he had lived his whole life.

"What time are you off Saturday night?" Lionel asked.

Gavin grabbed the handrail as they rounded the landing on C-deck. "After cleanup. Around ten."

"Come up to the first-class dining room—it's empty by then, and a few of us are going to have a card game."

Gavin glanced at the side of Lionel's face, then looked back at the stairs. "I've been coming up here." He pointed at the second-class library as they started downward again.

"You're going to read? When you could be playing poker?"

Gavin smiled and nodded. "I have to get to New York with all my pay. I can't expect my brother to support me."

Lionel slowed as they reached D-deck. "Come up if you change your mind. You can just sit with us; you don't have to play."

"I will, thanks."

Gavin watched as Lionel went into the first-class dining saloon. Through the open door Gavin saw that the room was still pretty full. The stewards were just beginning to clear away dirty dishes. Lionel's rakish grin disappeared, and his face became a mask of politeness as he turned and bent to whisper discreetly to a woman in a green silk gown.

Gavin shook his head as he pulled the door closed and turned to cross the landing. Going into the first-class pantry, he walked fast, rounding the corner by the neatly stacked crates of Waken & McLaughlin wine. The roast cook and one of the confectioners came through the galley door ahead of him. He stopped and turned sideways to let them pass. Neither man acknowledged his presence.

Gavin watched them walk away. He wasn't like Lionel. It was hard for him to smile at people who were rude to him, whether they were crew or passengers. He hurried into the galley, wishing he had been hired on as a dining room steward. They had it easier. A half hour after the last passenger left the dining saloons, the stewards would be changing the white tablecloths and setting the tables for the next meal. Then they would have a break.

"Hey! Gavin!"

Gavin turned to see Harry making his way across the crowded galley. His sharp-featured face was smudged with flour. He was already developing the short-strided, agile walk necessary to avoid collisions in the crowded, busy room.

Cooking never ceased here, except for a few hours in the middle of the night. The bakers began at three in the morning. The cooks started preparing breakfast early, then began lunch before the breakfast dishes were cleared. Dinner preparation sometimes started a day in advance, all the meals overlapping—only the chefs understood the schedule.

"Where have you been off to?" Harry asked, dodging a pantryman carrying an enormous, bloody roast. "You missed a chance to watch the pastry chef make éclairs."

Gavin shrugged. Harry wanted to be a chef someday and he rarely left the galley. "I went up for air," Gavin told him. "I just like to see the sky once in a while."

Harry nodded vaguely, turning when the sauce

chef bellowed out an order. Then his eyes focused on Gavin again. "What do you have to do now?"

Gavin made a face. "Wash a hundred and twenty pounds of new potatoes." Harry laughed, and Gavin pretended to take a swing at him. "It isn't funny. I hate the new potatoes worst of all. I can't even use the wire brushes because the skins tear so easily."

Harry grinned over his shoulder as he walked away. "Better you than me."

Gavin went to his basin. The pantrymen had already brought in the bags. He stared at the lettering. Whoever Charles Papas was, he sure raised a lot of potatoes.

"When do we raise anchor?" someone yelled behind him.

"Soon," the answer came. "Less than half an hour."

Gavin's throat tightened. There was no turning back now.

From the Author of
Infinity Ring Book Three

LISA McMANN

ARE YOU UNWANTED?